The chitinous snap of mandibles echoed against a pock-marked stone wall and a severed human head bounced into a puddle of blood. A helmet, knocked loose from the head, rolled round and round with a warbling clang, speeding up in its last few rotations before finally spinning to a stop. Next to the head, a man's body slumped to the ground with a soft thump.

Regdar wrenched his greatsword from a heap of oozing, gray-green flesh and turned toward the sound. Bodies lay scattered across the darkened floor. Blood ran in rivulets down the slanted passage until it collected again at the foot of a very large beast.

**From the creators of the
greatest roleplaying game ever
come tales of heroes fighting
monsters with magic!**

By T.H. Lain

The Savage Caves

The Living Dead

Oath of Nerull

City of Fire

The Bloody Eye

Treachery's Wake

Plague of Ice

The Sundered Arms

Return of the Damned

The Death Ray
(December 2003)

RETURN OF THE DAMNED

T.H. Lain

RETURN OF THE DAMNED

Distributed in the United States by Holtzbrinck Publishing.
Distributed in Canada by Fenn Ltd.

Distributed to the hobby, toy, and comic trade in the United States and Canada
by regional distributors.

Distributed worldwide by Wizards of the Coast, Inc. and regional distributors.

Printed in the U.S.A.

Cover art by Todd Lockwood & Sam Wood
First Printing: October 2003
Library of Congress Catalog Card Number: 2003100826

9 8 7 6 5 4 3 2 1

US ISBN: 0-7869-3003-9
UK ISBN: 0-7869-3004-7
620-17983-001-EN

U.S., CANADA,	EUROPEAN HEADQUARTERS
ASIA, PACIFIC, & LATIN AMERICA	Wizards of the Coast, Belgium
Wizards of the Coast, Inc.	T Hofveld 6d
P.O. Box 707	1702 Groot-Bijgaarden
Renton, WA 98057-0707	Belgium
+1-800-324-6496	+322-467-3360

Visit our web site at **www.wizards.com**

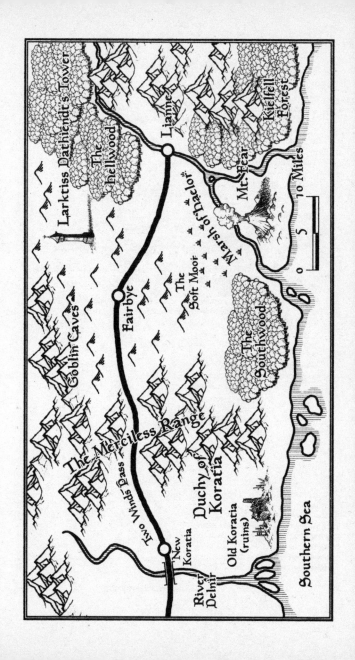

Prologue... Naull lay bleeding at the feet of the blackguard. She had saved her friends—saved Regdar—from death in the City of Fire by trapping the blackguard with a bead of force. The bead trapped Naull as well.

"That was quite a stunt, wizard," taunted the black-garbed figure standing over her.

Naull said nothing. She wanted to lash back at the horrid, armored woman, but in a few minutes both of them would die anyway. Naull was too badly hurt to spend her last moments in fruitless argument.

The City of Fire slipped steadily back into its pocket dimension. The portal to the Prime Material Plane was closed, and the city could no longer hold its position between the planes.

That wasn't the problem.

With the portal closed, the city would return completely to the Elemental Plane of Fire. Already flames lapped under the door frame and through cracks in the walls. The journey from one plane to the next didn't take long.

The force bead trapping both Naull and the blackguard would protect them for a while. Like all magic, eventually its power would fail. When that happened, Naull would be instantly incinerated.

It's not so bad, she thought. The end probably would come so fast she would feel nothing.

Behind her, the blackguard struggled with something inside her pack before pulling out a long, dirty-white staff.

Naull's curiosity got the best of her. "What is that?" she whispered.

The blackguard looked down at the injured wizard, but instead of the cruel scowl that Naull expected, the blackguard smiled.

"This is the thigh bone of a man I killed a few months ago," she said, gripping the rod with both hands. "I don't believe you knew him."

Naull cringed away, afraid the blackguard might find it amusing to beat her with it as a sacrifice to Hextor. "What are you going to do with it?"

"I'm going to break it," she said simply. With a crack, the blackguard snapped the bone in half against her own leg.

A blue-white spark crackled from the broken ends as a dark, red liquid poured from the hollowed-out bone. The blackguard's hands glowed with magical energy, and she reached for Naull.

The wizard squirmed away, but there was no room. The evil woman's hands clasped around Naull's arms. In the next moment, blackguard and wizard teleported away from the lapping flames of the Plane of Fire to a place of cold and intense darkness.

The City of Fire disappeared instantly. The effect was so startling that Naull first thought the blackguard had cast a spell to blind her. Then she felt the woman release her arms and shout the demonic word for light.

The smell of torches igniting filled Naull's nostrils. Light blazed in the wizard's eyes, and she squinted against the sudden, extreme change.

Naull lay on a floor of sand at the feet of the blackguard. The City of Fire was gone. They were now in a huge cavern. Torches on barbed poles formed a ring around the two women, outlining a large oval. Sooty whisps of smoke spiraled from the flames into darkness above. The light thrown by the torches was enough to illuminate everything inside the oval, but outside its circumference and up above, the light trailed off into nothing, seemingly swallowed by blackness.

The blackguard walked away. The sand crunched under her boots as she went, the sound doubling and redoubling in echoes across the dark chamber. As she reached the line of torches, she lifted one from the ground.

Naull pushed herself onto her knees to watch the blackguard as her torch receded into the darkness. The moving flame revealed more sandy ground, growing steadily smaller as the woman walked farther and farther away. Finally, it was no more than a ring of light flickering in the darkness.

After struggling to her feet, the wizard limped in the opposite direction. Her footsteps were loud against the packed sand in the quiet chamber. Naull watched over her shoulder, expecting the blackguard to give chase.

The ring of light in the distance continued on its course, apparently unconcerned by Naull's escape.

Crossing through the oval of torches, Naull turned her attention to the ground before her. She was only a few steps beyond the ring, but already the light grew weak. The farther she advanced, the darker the sand appeared, until she could see nothing but blackness beneath her feet.

Laughter from far behind stopped Naull in her tracks. Another ring of lights flared to life, these giving off the unmistakable blue-white glow of mage-lit stones. The floor on either side of Naull was fully illuminated, but before her, bare inches ahead of her feet, it plunged away into a deep chasm. She tottered and nearly lost her balance before her eyes could refocus.

Across the gap, the ground rose in steps like the seats of a coliseum.

Naull backed away from the edge and turned around. The magical lights revealed an enormous cavern. The oval of torches was ringed on three sides by the steep drop off. The coliseum seats followed the chasm all the way around the cavern, forming an immense gladiatorial arena.

She could not see the ceiling. It was too far above to be lit from the floor. Hanging from that vague darkness were heavy chains, and the chains suspended a dozen or more rusted, metal cages. Bones and rags stuck through the bars or swayed below the floor grates.

Directly across from Naull, far off on the fourth side of the arena, sat a huge throne. Jagged bits of obsidian formed the arms and legs. Above the seat back, inscribed into the stone, was the spiked gauntlet of Hextor, crushing in its grasp four wickedly barbed arrows.

The blackguard sat casually on the throne. "Now," she said quietly, her voice echoing and carried to Naull's ears by the shape of the cavern, "the question isn't so much how I will torture you, but how can I most benefit from it?"

3

One year later …

The chitinous snap of mandibles echoed against a pock-marked stone wall and a severed human head bounced into a puddle of blood. A helmet, knocked loose from the head, rolled round and round with a warbling clang, speeding up in its last few rotations before finally spinning to a stop. Next to the head, a man's body slumped to the ground with a soft thump.

Regdar wrenched his greatsword from a heap of oozing, gray-green flesh and turned toward the sound. Bodies lay scattered across the darkened floor. Blood ran in rivulets down the slanted passage until it collected again at the foot of a very large beast.

"Another umber hulk," grumbled Regdar. The creature stood at the end of the passage. At its feet lay the remains of an adventuring party—among them Regdar's close friend Whitman.

The fighter looked up at the beast with a burning hatred rising along his spine. Behind the creature, a few beams of natural light lancing down from the ceiling illuminated the dusty air, revealing a large chamber. From where Regdar stood, it looked as if the room might have been a bathhouse at one time.

The fighter sneered and lifted his blade. "Still hungry?" He took two quick steps forward. "Have a bite of this," he hollered. Then he launched himself into a charge down the hall, his greatsword raised overhead with both hands.

In just eight long steps, Regdar closed the distance between him and the half-ape, half-beetle monstrosity. The umber hulk flinched and stepped back. As Regdar swung his heavy blade, the tip scraped across the ceiling, showering sparks along its overhead arc.

The weapon sang as it swung free of the stone, but then it bounced sideways off the creature's thickly armored forearm. Regdar stumbled and struggled to keep hold of his sword.

The monster clacked its serrated mandibles. Its claws descended on the off-balance fighter. The first crashed against his breastplate. Sharp talons screeched, leaving deep creases in the gray metal. The second hit Regdar in the right shoulder, and the impact knocked him upright again.

The fighter balanced precariously on his toes for a second before the weight of his armor settled, and he landed flat on his feet with a noise like a tumbling pile of cook pots.

"Thanks," he grunted.

Regdar swung up his greatsword. The blade collided with the side of the creature's face and slashed open an oval-shaped organ Regdar could only assume was the monster's eye.

"How's that feel, you ugly dung muncher," he said. At the same time he readied the sword to attack again from what he hoped was now the creature's blind side.

The umber hulk reeled, black pulp gushing from its eye. Mandibles gnashed, and the air was filled with sounds of insectoid squeeking.

Regdar's next blow landed on the beast's arm. The thick hide made a popping noise as the blade bit through, then orange ooze pumped out in short bursts.

The umber hulk hissed and bent down into a crouch. It clicked its mandibles and scratched its claws along the stone floor. With one good eye it watched Regdar.

The right claw shot out lightning-quick. Regdar shifted to his right and evaded the swipe just in time to realize it was a feint. The creature's left claw thrust forward and slammed Regdar against the stone wall. His helmet banged hard against the rock, and he slid to the floor. His sword clattered and bounced, then settled to the ground with a dull chime.

Regdar was staggered but not dazed. Rolling away from the wall, he pushed himself to his knees and faced the drooling, bug-eyed monster.

"Is that the best you can do?" he said, spitting blood on the floor. He scooped up his sword and stepped back, steadying himself for the beast's next move.

The umber hulk's head lunged forward, snapping and biting at the fighter. The tips of its mandibles closed tightly around Regdar's left forearm.

The fighter grimaced and released his trapped hand's grip on the sword. Using only his right arm to wield the weapon, he sliced it across the monster's face, hoping to cut its remaining eye.

The sword was too long and the creature too close, but the danger made the umber hulk release Regdar's arm and skitter away beyond reach. Regdar pressed forward immediately. The tip of his sword missed the creature's eye, but the blade slid up the side of its head and carved a deep gouge in the carapace before dislodging what looked like an antenna.

The hulking vermin hunched down, then launched its considerable bulk forward again. Its body filled the passageway before landing on top of Regdar and crushing him to the floor. The fighter went down again with a clang, the monster lying on his legs, frantically clawing its way up his metal-encased body.

"This is all backward," muttered Regdar, struggling to pull himself out from under the foe. "Bugs don't squash people."

Mandibles gnashed in front of the fighter's face and drool splashed through his visor. Regdar had visions of his own head being snipped off and bouncing down the corridor when the creature spun around to face toward the old bathhouse. Regdar, too, twisted his head. Out of the corner of his eye, he saw movement and the glint of steel.

"Never was any good at sneaking!" came a gravelly voice.

Whitman, thought Regdar.

The umber hulk spun around in the passage and bounded off of Regdar. The fighter launched himself to his feet. Sure enough, at the end of the passage, hammer hefted over his shoulder, stood Whitman.

"Come and get me, you overgrown weevil," shouted the dwarf.

The umber hulk jumped forward and snapped its mandibles shut around Whitman's head. Regdar cringed at the sound of grinding metal.

A cloud of dust rolled out in front of the monster, heading in a line down the hall. It stopped at the opening to the bathhouse. A long gray beard swung in the clear air, and the cloud sprouted a dwarven head. Whitman had tumbled away, managing to keep his head and his hammer while losing only his helmet. The old dwarf swung his weapon over his shoulder again and hurled it at the beast.

Regdar closed the distance behind the umber hulk in two great steps. The tip of his sword bit into chitinous hide and plunged through. The monster convulsed and jolted forward. Whitman's hammer collided with the great beast's face, and its head recoiled backward. The monster looked as if it were dancing, undulating forward and back as blows struck it from both sides.

Regdar, his greatsword buried to the hilt in the creature's body, stepped back. His left arm was still bleeding from the umber hulk's earlier attack. He watched the creature jerk and twist as it struggled with its enormous claws to reach the sword in its back.

Whitman unhooked a throwing axe from his belt and reeled back. With a guttural cry, the dwarf let the weapon fly. The head of the axe crashed with a pop into the monster's skull. Large, yellow-gray curds burst out of the wound, sloshing over Whitman's hammer resting on the floor.

The beast roared with a sound that was part hiss, part shriek, then it slumped to the ground with its head twisted at an odd angle.

Regdar reached into his backpack with his good hand and pulled out a silver flask. Uncorking it with his teeth, the fighter downed the potion inside. At once the wound on his left arm glowed, scabbed over, and diminished in size.

Whitman climbed over the fallen umber hulk to retrieve his hammer.

"Ack," he groaned. "Brain juice . . . all over my hammer." He pulled a cloth from his belt and cleaned the sticky liquid and yellow-gray lumps from his weapon.

Regdar let the empty flask fall to the floor and grasped his sword with both hands. Putting his foot on the dead creature's back, he heaved the blade free with a loud, squishing sound.

"Could be worse," he consoled the dwarf. "Could be zombie brain juice."

Whitman chuckled. "Here I thought zombies had no brains."

"I hate to interrupt your witty banter," came a lisping voice from inside the bathhouse.

Whitman whipped around. Regdar raised his sword and leaped over the fallen monster to stand by the dwarf's side.

A hooded, black-robed figure stepped out of the shadows into a dust-filled beam of light. "That was my umber hulk, and nobody kills my monsters except me." The stranger lowered his hood to reveal a disfigured human face. A puckered, gray scar covered the

man's left eye and cheek. His upper lip was missing entirely, exposing his teeth and gums.

Extra air hissed out as he spoke words with a malformed
mouth. "Now I must kill you both." With that, he waved his hands
in the air and his voice rose to an unintelligible shout. Regdar
didn't recognize the words, but he knew well enough that they
meant magic.

Both fighters flung themselves sideways. A crackling bolt of
blue-white electricity shot from the disfigured wizard's fingers. It
jagged across the bathhouse and down the hallway. Despite their
quick reactions, Regdar and Whitman both were caught by the
snaking tendrils of electric power.

The bolt hit Regdar just below his hip. It passed right through
his metal armor and spread out to scorch his entire leg. Whitman
spun as he leaped for cover. That action saved his life. The bolt
missed his ear by mere inches. Instead it smashed into his shoulder and knocked the stout dwarf facefirst against the wall.

Smoke rose into the air, and the smell of burned flesh wafted
through the old bathhouse. The dark-robed wizard chuckled.

"Your turn," he said.

Whitman stood and hefted his hammer, shouting a single
Dwarvish word—the magical command that activated his boots of
speed. The old, gray-bearded dwarf bolted at the wizard. His feet
moved in a blur. The alarmed wizard stumbled backward, obviously caught off guard by the dwarf's surprising speed.

Whitman's first blow landed on the wizard's chest. It was powerful enough to shatter ribs, and the man staggered back. His arms
flailed at his sides as he struggled for balance. Gasping sounds
filled the room as he tried desperately to fill his lungs.

The dwarf's hammer fell again, this time smashing the wizard's
arm. Regdar heard bones snap under the impact. He let out a low
whistle as he hobbled on his scorched leg toward the two men.

Lowering his sword in his left hand, Regdar balled his right hand into a fist and punched the wizard square in the face. His gauntlet clanked against the robed man's mouth. The wizard's head snapped back from the impact, and pieces of broken teeth clattered across the tiled floor.

The wizard collapsed to his knees.

Regdar rested his sword blade at the base of the wizard's neck. "Surrender."

The dark-robed man sat on the floor, probing the bloody holes in his smile with his finger. He looked up at Regdar, shrugged, then put his hands into his robe.

"Keep those where I can see them," threatened Regdar, and he applied some downward pressure on the blade.

The wizard smiled. Blood dripped from holes in his gums and ran down his chin. He withdrew his hands from his robes, but he held a small, pink ball of goo between two fingers. The substance flashed then disintegrated. Regdar squinted involuntarily to protect his eyes. The wizard lisped out two quick words, and he disappeared.

Shaking his head, Regdar growled. The sound echoed off the walls of the old bathhouse. Too late, the fighter sliced with his sword where the wizard had been kneeling. His greatsword struck nothing but the floor.

Regdar looked to Whitman. The dwarf shrugged, and both men scanned the room, their weapons at the ready.

In the corner, a cluster of glowing, blue-white orbs appeared. They floated in mid-air, casting an eerie glow on the darkened chamber. Both fighters stepped forward before the magical missiles lifted from where they hovered and streaked toward them. The lights swirled and blurred, then smashed into the human and the dwarf.

Regdar heard a short yelp escape his lips as the skin on his chest sizzled and popped. Despite the pain, the fighter charged toward the corner, his eyes trained on the apparently empty spot where the orbs had appeared.

In his mind, Regdar imagined the hooded man standing before him, casting the spell and dodging away. Lunging to his left as he reached the corner, the big fighter leaned into his strike, praying his hunch was correct.

His greatsword met resistance in what looked like thin air, then a flood of bright-red blood gushed across the blade.

Whitman, only a step behind, zeroed in on the freshly opened wound and swung his hammer in a flat arc. The head of the weapon connected with something that made a sickening crunch. Regdar's sword was pulled sideways by an invisible force. More blood gushed down the blade, then the wizard materialized in a heap on the floor.

Regdar pulled his sword free and wiped the blade on the dead man's robe. "So many bad men, so little time."

Then the big fighter sheathed his sword and walked into the darkness at the other side of the room.

Whitman balanced his hammer on his shoulder and looked down at the fallen wizard. He shook his head.

"Sweet gifts of Pelor," shouted Regdar. "Come take a look at this." He pulled off his helmet and let it drop. Loosening his backpack, he flung it to the floor in front of him and dropped to his knees in a pile of gold coins, gems, and books.

"Would you look at this," he said, picking up handfuls of coins and letting them slip through his fingers. The cascading treasure made a pleasant, jingling sound as it landed on the jumbled pile. "This guy and his umber hulks must have cleaned out most of the ruins."

Whitman lowered himself to the floor beside Regdar and began scooping swag into his backpack. He smiled and slapped his friend on the shoulder.

Regdar did the same, packing as much as he could carry. Between scoops of gold coins and huge jewels, the fighter lifted a rather plain-looking amulet with a single, archaic rune inscribed on its surface. Shrugging, he looped its leather band over his head and let the amulet hang from his neck. He smiled down at it momentarily, then resumed filling his backpack.

Several handfuls into the pile, Regdar uncovered a jewel-encrusted flask. He lifted it up to get a better look. Holding it out into one of the few beams of light that penetrated this far into the ruins, he examined the vessel. The opening at its top was sealed with red wax. Along its edges, embedded gems formed pictures of beasts and men, all fighting against each other. The scenes entranced Regdar, and he stared at the flask as if concentrating intently.

The bottle felt strange in his hand. It was heavy, much heavier than any potion the fighter had held. It wasn't the weight that concerned him. It was more of an impulse. Regdar felt as if the bottle might burst open at any moment, as if whatever was inside the flask was too big to be contained in such a small flagon, and if it stayed there much longer, the sides might just crack apart.

Regdar put his hand on top of the flask. The pressure inside the bottle seemed so great, Regdar thought the cork might pop out on its own. He grabbed hold of it with his thumb and forefinger.

Whitman dropped his fleshy palm on his friend's shoulder. "Perhaps we should leave that for the duke to deal with," he said.

Regdar shook his head, then looked down at the bottle again. "Yes," he said. "I think that would be best." He looked back up at the dwarf and smiled. "I don't know what got into me."

Shaking his head, Regdar shoved the flask into his backpack.

2

Six months earlier …

The blackguard stood at the edge of her arena. In the middle, two tattooed men fought. Both were stripped to the waist, barefoot, and bleeding. Each had a short sword and a buckler. They were winded from fighting for nearly an hour.

On their chests, heaving up and down with each exaggerated breath, were three words written in the infernal language of the Abyss—and the symbol of Hextor himself. The god of battle had smiled upon them, and these men, in turn, had dedicated their lives to him, showing their devotion by tattooing their bodies with the image of their god.

The blackguard read those words to herself now: war; conflict; destruction. They were words she could take to heart.

In the arena, a sword clanked off a buckler, and one of the warriors fell to the ground with a blade in his gut.

The stands erupted in cheers. The blackguard smiled as she looked out at nearly a thousand men, each shirtless, each carrying the mark of Hextor on his chest.

The victorious warrior stood over his wounded victim, looking to the blackguard, waiting patiently for a sign.

The crowd chanted, "Finish him! Finish him! Finish him!"

The blackguard slipped her sword from its sheath. The chamber went silent. This was her favorite part. Lifting the blade high in the air, she looked at the warriors in the middle—one bleeding, one wanting blood.

"Send him to Hextor," she said, and she lowered her blade.

The poised warrior did not hesitate before plunging the end of his short sword into the man and ending his life.

The blackguard turned and walked back to her throne. Sitting down, she watched two more men drag the corpse to the edge of the chasm and push it over. Then they returned to the center of the arena, nodded to each other, and began fighting.

A robed man stepped from behind the throne and prostrated himself before the woman seated on it, his face touching the ground.

"Mistress," he said with a lisp, "we have located the bottle."

The blackguard nearly stood up. "Where?"

"In the duchy of New Koratia," answered the robed man, "in some ruined catacombs off the River Delnir."

"The Herald of Hell has smiled upon us," she said, looking over her shoulder at the fist of Hextor.

"Yes, my mistress." The man kept his face to the dirt. "What is your desire?"

Behind him, one of the cultist's swords caught the other man under the chin, taking his head off in a single stroke.

The blackguard templed her fingers. "It is time to move the cult to the duchy of New Koratia," she said. "I want you to personally undertake the retrieval of the bottle."

The man sat up. As he did, the cowl of his robe fell back to reveal a puckered, gray scar over his left eye and cheek. When he smiled, his ruined lips parted to show his teeth and most of his gums.

"As you command, my mistress."

Present Day ...

Regdar dragged his overloaded pack out of the tunnel and into the fresh air. The sun was just coming up.

"Every time we go down into the ruins of Old Koratia I lose track of time," mused the fighter. He let his pack settle to the ground and stood up, stretching.

"Then you wouldn't make much of a dwarf," replied Whitman. He lowered his load as well to adjust his armor and hammer. "Ain't no sunrise in the mines."

Regdar shook his arms, then hefted the sack over his shoulder. "Speaking of that, there's something I've been meaning to ask you."

Whitman blew out a deep breath and grunted as he lifted his heavy treasure bag. "What would that be?"

Both men started toward the walled city of New Koratia in the near distance.

"Well," started Regdar, "exactly what kind of name is Whitman for a dwarf?"

The dwarf grunted. "You got a problem with my name?"

"No. No." Regdar smirked. "It's just that it—"

"That it what?" growled the dwarf.

"That it sounds like a human name—one you might expect of a banker or one of the duke's personal advisors. A smart man, not a grumbling, old dwarf." Regdar laughed so hard he almost lost his load.

"Laugh it up, meat head." Whitman shifted his pack. "At least I'm not named Regdar."

"What's wrong with Regdar?" asked the human.

"It sounds like a human name—one you might expect of a big, dumb guy whose solution to everything is to bash it to bits." The dwarf laughed. "On second thought, I take it back. It suits you."

"Very funny, little man." Regdar snorted.

Whitman laughed again.

"But I'm serious," interjected the big fighter. "I've never met another dwarf with a human-sounding name."

Whitman cocked his head and looked over his pack at Regdar. He nodded. "If you must know—"

Regdar stopped walking.

Whitman did the same and looked gravely up at the big fighter. "I was raised by a human family until the age of sixteen. They found me wrapped in a blanket, next to a stump in the woodlands not far from Fairbye."

"What were you doing out there?"

"Don't know." The dwarf shrugged. "Guess I was abandoned."

Regdar was puzzled. "How did the human family find you? Those woodlands aren't exactly well-traveled."

"They were part of a traveling circus—tumblers, acrobats, you know. They were getting ready to camp for the night. Guess they were starting a new show the next morning."

Regdar smiled. "So that's where you learned to roll around on the floor like that."

The dwarf scowled. "You call it rolling around on the floor. I call it an art form."

Regdar laughed. "Whatever."

Whitman continued with his story, ignoring the jibe. "It was my human parents who named me—after a great-great grand-father who—" Whitman rolled his eyes— "had served as an advisor to the king."

"Ha!" shouted Regdar. "I knew it."

Whitman narrowed his eyes at his friend. "Did you now?"

"Well, didn't I just say Whitman sounded like the name of one of the duke's advisors?" Regdar smiled ear to ear.

"Proud of yourself then, are you?" Whitman turned and continued toward New Koratia.

Regdar hurried to catch up, still smiling. "But I've heard some of the other dwarves in the barracks call you 'Gruble'."

Whitman nodded. "That's just a nickname." He turned toward Regdar. "For those who don't like Whitman."

Regdar's smile faded. "I meant no offense."

The dwarf scowled for a moment, then broke into a gap-toothed grin. "I know lad," he said. "I'm just messing with you."

The two fighters stepped up to the guardhouse and were greeted by a dozen or more rowdy soldiers. Regdar and Whitman lowered their packs.

"Welcome home, Captain," shouted a burly, human man with a tattoo of a longsword on his forearm. He slapped Regdar on the shoulder.

A tall, muscular elf stepped through the crowd and lifted one of the heavy sacks.

"Let me help you back to the barracks," he said. "The duke will be wanting to see you." He looked Whitman over from head to toe. "And I'm sure he doesn't want a dirty dwarf in his personal chambers."

Whitman looked up. "I may be dirty, Tasca, but at least I don't smell like elf."

"They're at it again," said the big human with the tattoo. He rolled his eyes.

Someone grabbed the other pack, and Regdar, Whitman, and a handful of others walked down the street toward the River Delnir. The river bisected the city into two roughly equal parts. The road the men walked on cut New Koratia in the opposite direction, creating four distinctly different quarters. The southwest part of the city was known as the Dark Quarter—the part of the city where thieves and brigands roamed freely. Several years previous, the duke saw fit to move the army barracks there. Regdar assumed it was to deter the criminal element from overstepping the bounds. Whatever the rationale, the soldiers' presence did little to instill law and order. Crime still thrived in the darkened alleyways and back streets of the Dark Quarter. Now, however, as a matter of survival, the criminals had grown better at hiding, sneaking, and avoiding the city watch. If anything, the army's presence made the thieves better at their trade.

At the end of the road, where the cobblestones met the rushing waters of the Delnir, the soldiers turned in to their barracks. Two sentries at the entrance shouted to their returning captain and his dwarf companion.

Regdar entered the barracks and went immediately to his bunk. Doffing his chestplate, gauntlets, and vambraces, the fighter collapsed on the soft bed. The privileges of being an officer in the duke's army were not lost on the fighter. Though he didn't need the extra comforts, he couldn't deny how good it felt to rest his tired body.

He must have fallen asleep, because what seemed like only a few seconds passed before he was awakened by a loud noise. The veteran leaped to his feet, his greatsword in hand.

"Easy, big fella," calmed Whitman. "It's just the duke."

Regdar shook himself awake and lowered his sword. A well-muscled, gray haired man wearing full ornamental platemail and a magenta velvet cape stepped through the door.

Regdar dropped to one knee and bowed his head. Whitman, Tasca, and the other soldiers did the same.

"Rise. Please, rise," commanded the duke. He smiled as he crossed the room. He walked over and placed his hand on Regdar's shoulder. "I'm glad for your safe return."

"Thank you, my lord," replied Regdar, standing rigidly before Duke Christo Ramas.

The duke nodded, then walked over to Whitman and shook the

old dwarf's hand. "Tell me," he said, "did you retrieve it?" He looked from Whitman to Regdar.

Regdar nodded.

Duke Christo Ramas clapped his hands once. "Excellent. Let me see it."

Regdar crossed to his backpack and dumped most of the contents on the wooden floor. Coins and gems made a clanking racket as they tumbled out, then the jewel-encrusted flask rolled free and came to rest on top of the other treasure.

The duke's eyes grew wide, and he got down on his knees to lift the vessel from the ground. He spun the bottle in his hands, examined the jeweled patterns, and inspected the wax seal to make sure it was intact. He breathed a relieved sigh and stood up.

"You've done good work, men," he commended. The duke made eye contact with all the soldiers in the room, smiling. "Tonight we celebrate the return of our heroes—" he nodded at both Whitman and Regdar and hoisted the bottle overhead— "and the return of the bottle to my custody."

The blackguard paced the floor of her new chambers. The personal effects of the previous lord of this castle still lay in disarray around the room. She kicked a dwarf's skull out of her way as she walked.

"Necromancers."

The door opened and a trio of men entered. Two wore black splintmail and helms. Between them was a third man wearing dark blue robes. His head was bare and shaved, his eyes open but unseeing—pearly white orbs that scanned the room but took in nothing. He carried his hands hidden inside his vestments, and his head rolled from side to side as he walked escorted by the armored figures.

The group stopped a few feet from the blackguard, and one of the warriors stepped forward.

"Do you have news of the recovery effort?" she asked.

"We do, Mistress," he said.

"Go on."

The man straightened himself as best he could, inhaled deeply, then said, "The mission is a failure. The bottle has been stolen and both the wizard and his umber hulks have been slain."

The blackguard screeched. Her sword whipped from its sheath and rang as it sliced through the man's armor. Blood sprayed across the floor where the body tumbled down.

The blackguard turned to the remaining armored man. "Is this true?"

The other warrior stepped forward without hesitation. "Yes, Mistress."

"And you, mage," she said, nodding at the robed man, "what do you know of this?"

The bald, sightless man withdrew his hands from his robes. "I know who has the bottle now."

The blackguard lowered her sword. "Show me."

The robed man knelt down and drew several sigils in the dust on the floor. He recited an incantation, and a white globe formed between his outstretched hands. On the surface of the globe pictures formed, and the pictures moved.

The blackguard leaned over and stared into the globe. A pair of fighters took shape—one dwarven, one human.

"Regdar," she said. "Well, well. Perhaps I have found a use for the wizard bitch after all."

The duke's estate rested squarely in the middle of an island that split the rushing waters of the River Delnir. Just as the river split the city of New Koratia in two, so did the island split the river. Bridges from both the east and west sides of the city rose over the flowing water to connect the island to the rest of New Koratia.

Night had fallen, and at the very center of the island, the ducal palace was lit up with several hundred torches. A band played on a stage at the middle of the festival. Tables had been set and a feast laid out in the center courtyard. Regdar sat next to Whitman and Tasca—uncomfortable in their shiny, if ineffective, dress uniforms—while they ate their meal.

"Hey, Regdar," said Tasca, looking across the courtyard, "I think you have an admirer."

Regdar looked to the elf. "Where?"

Tasca pointed with his chin, and the big fighter followed with his eyes. Near the eastern wall, seated next to the duke, an attractive, young lass smiled.

Regdar forced a smile, then conscientiously focused on his food. "The duke's daughter," he said.

The elf elbowed Regdar in the ribs. "What are you waiting for? Go talk to her."

"I have no interest in talking about the politics of court with a pretentious, royal brat." The big fighter pushed another spoonful of stewed duck into his mouth. "Besides, I'm enjoying the music."

"Leave the poor boy alone," scolded Whitman. "You know Regdar's still blubbering over the one who got away." The old dwarf smiled and downed a big gulp of ale.

Regdar slammed his spoon to the table. "Naull didn't 'get away', all right? She's dead! Do you get it? Dead." He looked up at the other two and shook his head. "Can't either of you shut up for a few minutes?"

"It was the elf's fault," accused Whitman.

"Why is it my fault?" replied Tasca.

"Because it's always your fault, you overgrown wood sprite," Whitman mumbled.

Tasca turned back to his ale. "At least I'm not a tunneling rodent," he muttered.

"Will you two—" Regdar stopped when he noticed a gnome in ceremonial armor approaching. "Captain Gohem Masters." Regdar stood as he greeted the gnome. "Shouldn't you be guarding the duke?" he said with a grin as he shook the small man's tiny hand.

"From what I hear, you have enough trouble doing your own job, let alone mine, Captain Regdar," replied the gnome. "Besides, I am protecting him." He held up his hand, displaying an unobtrusive but heavy-looking golden ring.

"With expensive jewelry?" teased Regdar.

"Precisely." The gnome smiled. "With this ring I can cast a shield spell on the duke from anywhere. If he's in danger, I can protect him instantly."

"When did you become so fancy?" quipped Whitman.

The gnome stepped over and shook the dwarf's hand. "When I became the head of the duke's elite guard."

"Very fancy indeed," said Tasca, taking another bite of his meal while admiring the ring.

The gnome laughed. "If I didn't know you so well, Tasca, I might have thought I detected a hint of jealousy."

"Ah, you know elves, Gohem," interjected the dwarf. "If they're not looking at themselves in the mirror, they're coveting your coin sack."

"I see you two haven't changed," said the gnome. "If you're done with your meal, Regdar, the duke would like to have a word with you." He turned to Whitman and Tasca as they started getting up. "In private."

Regdar grinned at the other two, then turned to Captain Masters. "Lead the way."

Whitman and Tasca returned to their meals.

The gnome traversed the courtyard, dodging torches, dancing maidens, and drunken merchants. Regdar followed as closely as he could, but Gohem's small stature allowed him a much freer path through the crowd. Near the eastern wall, still seated, Duke Christo Ramas watched them approach.

As they drew closer, the duke waved his hand, and several people standing near him, his daughter included, moved away, leaving only a pair of armed guards in the duke's immediate vicinity.

"Regdar," he said as the two men came into earshot, "how are you enjoying the feast?"

Regdar lowered himself onto one knee and bowed. "As usual, the meat is exquisite, and the ale cool and frothy." He stood and smiled. "Please give my compliments to your chef."

"I'll do that." He turned to Captain Masters and nodded. The gnome made a whistling sound, and the soldiers guarding the duke disappeared into the crowd, leaving the two men alone.

"Please," said the duke, indicating a place at the bench with an open hand, "sit down."

Regdar did as he was told.

The duke took a sip of ale from an ornamental stone mug, then set it on the table with a resounding thud.

"You know, when I was in the military, I used to hate these parties," said the duke.

Regdar was surprised. "Why, my lord?"

"Because those damned dress uniforms are so itchy and stiff," replied the duke. "No matter how much ale I drank, I never got comfortable. I was always glad to take it off at the end of the night."

Both men laughed.

The relaxed demeanor of the duke put Regdar at ease. "May I ask you a question, Duke?"

"Of course."

"The bottle we retrieved. It felt so ... unnatural ... strange...." The big fighter fished for the right words. "It was as if it was trying to speak to me," he blurted. He looked to the duke then shrugged. "What is—"

The duke cut him off with a stern look and a shake of his head. "Let's just say, it's important that it stays out of the wrong hands. It's best if we leave it at that."

Regdar nodded, a little irritated at being brushed off.

"Now can I ask you a question?"

"Of course, my lord," Regdar replied.

"Drop the formal crap for now, Regdar." The duke sat up straight. "Tonight we talk like soldiers, fighting men enjoying their ale together." He pushed a mug toward Regdar, who scooped it up.

"All right, Christo." He raised his mug. "What do you want to know?"

The duke's smile turned into a grimace. "Why do you keep volunteering for these suicide missions?"

Regdar wiped froth from his upper lip. "I didn't know you considered my missions suicidal."

"What else could I consider them?" replied the duke. "Sending a small group of men into the ruins below the city . . ." He shrugged. "If that bottle hadn't been so important, I wouldn't have asked anyone to go down there."

"Would you have rather sent someone else, someone with less experience?"

"Frankly, yes," replied the duke. "Regdar, you are a terrific soldier and a fantastic fighter—"

"So what's the problem?" Regdar raised his voice. "I got the job done."

The duke chuckled. "Yes, you did. Calm down for a minute and listen to me." He looked Regdar in the eyes. "You're a captain, Regdar. Anybody can smash a door and kill an orc, but it takes a real soldier to lead men into battle." He sighed deeply and patted Regdar on the shoulder. "I didn't make you a captain so you could get yourself killed by volunteering for every dangerous mission. I made you a captain because you're an excellent leader. Your job is to command others and send *them* on dangerous missions. If you're gone, who's going to keep order in the barracks? Who's going to see that the new recruits are properly trained and motivated? Who's going to inspire the men to defend our homes?"

"I understand," said Regdar, looking down at the table.

"Being a soldier is never going to be without risks," the duke added. "Now that you're a captain, you need to be careful about which ones you take on yourself."

Regdar was silent, deep in thought.

"Look." Duke Ramas opened his hands wide. "This wizard you faced in the ruins isn't going to be the last. There will always be another threat to New Koratia just waiting around the bend, and I need commanders who can handle the troops. Losing soldiers in battle is unavoidable, but losing valuable captains to an umber hulk under the city isn't. You see that, don't you?"

Regdar looked up from his ale and nodded. "Yes, Duke, I do."

"Good." The duke smiled and lifted his mug. "To your successful mission." He took a big drink.

Regdar looked up into the sky. Perhaps being a captain wasn't what he wanted after all. He sighed.

A high-pitched whistle shrieked over the barrier wall to the north, followed quickly by a massive fireball.

Regdar launched himself from the bench and dived on top of the duke.

The fireball smashed into the table, turning it instantly into an inferno and vaporizing Regdar's ale.

Ladies in fine dresses and merchants in feathered hats ran every which way. Screams echoed inside the protective walls of the duke's keep. The delightful celebration dissolved into chaos as New Koratia came under attack.

Regdar lifted himself off of the duke while pulling splinters out of his ceremonial uniform and feeling his exposed flesh for other wounds.

"Damn," hollered the duke, still flat on the ground, "where did that come from?"

"We're under attack from the north," answered Captain Masters, who had appeared suddenly after the blast.

"Why didn't the guards sound the alarm?" barked the duke.

"The attackers came down the river on a raft." The gnome waved two soldiers over to help lift the duke from the ground. "No one saw them coming. They just appeared out of nowhere."

The duke got to his feet and brushed himself off.

Regdar shook his head to clear the ringing from his ears while he listened to what Captain Masters had to say.

The gnome straightened up to his full height. "We need to get you to safety, my lord. They're attacking the keep directly." He ushered the duke toward the inner keep. "They're on the other side of that wall." He pointed to the north, indicating the corner of the courtyard not more than a hundred feet from the duke.

Regdar didn't wait to hear any more. He sprinted across the courtyard, dodging or bowling over panicked guests on his way to Whitman and Tasca. The two fighters met their captain halfway, hammer and sword already drawn.

Regdar shouted to be heard above the screaming and chaos. "Whitman, you help direct the guests back inside the inner keep. Then find Krunk and meet us at the north wall."

The dwarf grunted and jogged away, herding panicked partyers to safety.

"Tasca," Regdar shouted, "have you seen Clemf?"

The elf nodded. "Right behind you."

Regdar turned around. The big man with the longsword tattooed on his forearm stood behind him. He wore the same military dress uniform as the rest of the soldiers, but the sleeves were torn off, exposing his enormous biceps.

"So much for formality," mumbled Regdar. He grabbed the big man by the shoulder. "Follow me."

Another huge fireball screamed over the north wall and impacted the stage in the middle of the courtyard where the bards had been performing. Flaming splinters of broken instruments fluttered in every direction. All three men ducked to avoid the missiles.

"What do they have against music?" asked Clemf.

Regdar looked at the big man and shook his head. "Come on," he yelled over the roaring flames. Then he ran toward the north wall.

The noise from the crowd had died down now that most of the guests were safely inside the inner keep. Only soldiers or guards remained in the courtyard.

The top of the wall buzzed with the sound of bowstrings. At the farthest northern point, where two walls met to form the top corner of the diamond-shaped courtyard, two armed guards stood near a wooden sally port. Regdar ran up behind them with Tasca and Clemf in tow.

"What's the story, Plathus?" he asked.

A tall elf wearing the colors of the duke's elite guard and peering out through a bolt hole in the wooden door answered. "There's a raft full of soldiers preparing to climb the wall," he said. "As you've probably guessed, they're accompanied by wizards."

"How many wizards?"

"Two that I can see."

Regdar turned around. Whitman had arrived with Krunk—a white-bearded dwarf with a mace in one hand and a symbol of Pelor in the other.

Regdar smiled as he looked at the four men assembled behind him. "You know the first rule of combat."

"Kill the wizard," replied all four in unison.

Plathus moved aside and Regdar nodded. The heavy wooden crossbeam complained as it was drawn open. When another fireball screamed across the wall, the door to the sally port swung inward with a loud creak.

Five soldiers of the duke's army of New Koratia dashed out of the keep and straight into a wall of black-clad soldiers. The tiny northern embankment of the duke's island swarmed with them. Their raft was made from logs as big around as Regdar was tall. If he had to guess, he would have estimated the thing could hold as many as forty or even fifty heavily armed soldiers. Right now, he didn't want to think about that. It was him and four of his best men, in their fancy dress uniforms, against a force almost ten times their size wearing spiked scale mail.

The odds didn't look good.

A glob of magical energy sizzled past Regdar's head to smash into the wall of the keep. The stone where it impacted smoked and hissed.

That really didn't look good.

Regdar's greatsword came out of its scabbard in a flash, and metal rang all around. The melee ensued in earnest as the small band of fighters clashed with the invading army and their wizards.

Whitman's hammer smashed into a black-clad chest plate, and he tumbled forward into another opponent. The first man doubled over, his collapsed armor squeezing the life out of him. The second stumbled and tripped over the dwarf's well-placed kick. A third stepped up, preparing to take a swing at the now-prone dwarf.

Tasca lunged forward. The blade of his rapier glittered in the moonlight. Its tip slipped between interlocking metal plates into soft flesh. The impaled man gave out a tremendous cough, spat blood, then let his upraised sword fall harmlessly to the ground next to Whitman. The dwarf rolled away from the tumbling body.

Clemf dived into the battle as well. The big, tattooed human waved his bastard sword like a wand, leveling black-armored fighters with each swing. He moved exceptionally fast for a large man. Each lunge covered twice the ground a dwarf might in the same number of steps.

Krunk waded in behind Clemf, clearing away with his mace those left in the wake of the fast-moving human. Though his legs were short, his arms were mighty, and a large, oval clearing appeared rapidly in the middle of the opposing soldiers' line around the huge barbarian and the dwarf.

Another fireball exploded inside the keep—this one on top of the wall. Bricks and flaming limbs rained down the embankment. The fires were extinguished as they cascaded across the damp ground, and the debris made squishy, thumping noises as it came to rest. Regdar was far into the enemy line, but he could hear bricks—or what he hoped were bricks—landing behind him.

Some of the black-clad attackers were not as fortunate, and were hammered to the ground by the grisly rain.

As the flaming downpour tapered off, Regdar's greatsword swept round in a whistling arc. It smacked aside a defending long-sword and cut a deep wound into the belly of the man before Regdar. The soldier squealed as he lowered his sword and fell to his knees, bloody hands desperately grasping at his guts in a vain attempt to keep them from spilling onto the ground. Regdar stepped past the screaming attacker and kept fighting.

Two more soldiers lunged forward from both sides at once. Regdar retreated, knocking aside one blade while trying to be mindful of the wounded man behind him. A sharp pain in his right hamstring forced Regdar down onto one knee.

The gutted man behind Regdar had fallen sideways, but his sword, still tightly gripped, was poised with its point in the air. That point was now jabbed into the back of Regdar's leg. Pain shot up through the limb, through his lower back, and right on into his shoulder. Regdar managed to keep hold of his sword as he let out a roar that echoed above the sounds of battle.

The sword slipped free of Regdar's leg, and the searing pain gave way to a dull throb. Despite the pain and loss of balance, he managed to drop to the ground in time to duck beneath the swift, flat swing of another sword that was aimed at his neck. Three heavily armored men approached from the direction of the riverbank.

Regdar hopped backward and bashed away two blades with one swing, but the exertion sent tremendous pain ripping up his leg. He continued hobbling backward, hoping the attackers would be slowed by their heavy armor in their ascent up the slope.

The fastest of the soldiers lunged for Regdar's injured leg. The blade stabbed deep into the front of Regdar's thigh and scraped against the bone. Nearly blinded by the pain, he reeled back and released one hand from his greatsword to steady himself.

Expecting Regdar to fall, the enemy fighter sprang forward with his blade raised high. To his shock, Regdar didn't fall. Instead, the heavy, steel pommel of a greatsword gripped in a massive fist smashed into the man's helmet, crunching the dark steel inward against the side of his head. Blood gushed from the faceplate of the collapsed helm.

The injured man gurgled out a panicked scream. On his knees he clawed at the ruined helmet with both hands. Eventually he pried it loose with a soft, ripping sound from the hair that was tightly pinched in the metal. Blood poured out of the metal pot, and the man's face seemed strangely elongated.

The other two men stepped blithely past their comrade with the broken face. Regdar hopped away while trying to put pressure on at least one of the wounds in his leg, but the two pursuers were gaining ground. With no good choices left, Regdar knew he had to stand his ground. Falling in the fight would be far better than being stabbed in the back trying to escape. He turned and pointed his greatsword at the oncoming attackers.

The first one attacked high. Regdar parried the swing easily with an upward strike. It was only a feint. The second attack came low. A less experienced warrior would have died there and then, but Regdar knew the danger. His leg seemed afire as he shifted his weight to block the second blade. Steel rang against steel, and a terrific growl roared through Regdar's clenched teeth. Still, the pain was too much. The doubly wounded leg collapsed despite Regdar's will and toppled him off balance. The next attack cut a large gash in Regdar's shoulder as he fell to the ground.

Despite the pain, Captain Regdar's mind was crystal clear. He rolled onto his back in the mud and gripped his greatsword in his right hand. Holding the weapon defensively over his chest, he looked up at the two black-clad soldiers. He couldn't see their faces through their helms, but after a hundred battles, he knew how they would look. There was just room for one deep breath and one powerful, perfectly timed swing. The blade whistled in a level arc just inches above the ground.

Another fireball exploded above the keep. The flash of light lit the ground and the red spray arcing out behind Regdar's glinting blade where it sliced cleanly through three ankles. One soldier toppled to the ground, screaming and clutching at the stumps of his shins. The second was made of tough stuff. He bellowed off his pain and anger, stamped his bleeding left ankle into the soft ground, and somehow kept his balance.

Now Regdar could see the man's eyes grow narrow through the helmet's faceplate as he glared down at him. The blade rose, the eyes grew wide, and the sword plunged down. In that second, Regdar hoped that a cleric might find him before his soul departed forever. He heard the sound of a blade slicing flesh and saw the sword drive deep—into the mud beneath his armpit!

Regdar craned his neck. The black-clad soldier fell to his knees, then collapsed across Regdar's chest. Behind him stood Tasca, his rapier dripping the dead man's blood.

A pair of strong hands slid under Regdar's shoulders and struggled to drag him from under the slain enemy.

"Use your feet, you big sack of meat," chided Whitman from behind Regdar. "You're not the only one who's hurt, you know."

Regdar breathed a sigh of relief and lifted with his uninjured leg. Once supported by Whitman, the big fighter looked around.

At least fifteen of the attacking soldiers lay dead in the mud along the small, northern embankment around the sally port. The wizards still lived, however, along with at least thirty more black-clad soldiers, all of whom seemed to be granting Regdar and his men a wide, clear space. Farther down the wall, some had managed to secure a pair of heavy ladders against the bastion, but their attention was fixed on Regdar and his irregulars.

A loud crash turned Regdar, Tasca, and Whitman to their left. An attacker tumbled sideways down the slope and splashed into the water. Clemf burst through the space where the soldier had been standing. The burly, tattooed human bulled his way toward Regdar, slashing and clubbing anyone impetuous enough to try barring his way. Clemf's dress uniform, already missing its arms even before the battle, now hung in tatters. He looked like a wild man raised by wolves, dressed in the rags of his formerly civilized clothing. Cuts and bruises covered his body. Sweat drenched his brow and dripped from his limbs. With an enormous swing, he cleaved one more soldier in two, then stepped up next to his three compatriots.

"Where's Krunk?" he yelled, turning his back on Regdar and menacing the approaching soldiers.

"I thought he was with you," replied Regdar. He scanned the battlefield. Out of the corner of his eye, he caught sight of the dwarf. Krunk was lifting himself onto the raft, directly beside the wizards. "There!" Regdar shouted, pointing. "Krunk made it to the raft."

As if they'd heard Regdar's words, both wizards turned to face the dwarf with their spells.

"Damn." Regdar hopped forward, trying to keep weight off his injured leg while preparing to cut a path through the enemy soldiers between him and the raft.

Whitman and Tasca rushed ahead of him toward the advancing line of enemy troops. Clemf stepped beside Regdar, and the four men moved as one. Before they had advanced two steps, however, the enemy soldiers surrounded them.

"This is all your fault, elf," Whitman declared as he stood back to back with Tasca.

"If it wasn't for me, you'd be dead now, you brash, tumbling fool," responded Tasca. "Now shut up and hit something with that hammer for once."

The circle of swords surrounding Regdar and the others grew deeper and tighter. The tip of a blade flashed out and caught Regdar across the forearm. He pulled back, swearing at his slow reaction and his bleeding arm. The attacker regretted his bold action a moment later when Clemf's sword sliced through his knee.

With the sounds of battle ringing all around, Regdar studied the slowly enclosing noose surrounding them. Krunk was still on the raft, his mace raised high in the air. He didn't move, and the wizards had again turned their backs on him. Regdar realized the dwarf was frozen in time.

A dull blow to Regdar's chest brought his attention back to his immediate danger. He'd been saved from what might have been a very serious slash by Tasca's parry, which turned the attacker's blade sideways.

"Well boys," Regdar yelled, "it's been an honor and a privilege." His greatsword jabbed through the eye slit in a black helmet and punched through brain, skull, and steel at the back of the helmet. The blade bit tightly into the metal and refused to break loose when Regdar yanked it back, so he pulled the weapon sideways and hammered the protruding tip through a second man's breastplate. The weight of two dead men bore the weapon toward the ground.

From somewhere a mace crashed down on Regdar's blade and tore the grip from his hands. Bodies pressed forward, waving weapons toward the fighter. Before he could be overwhelmed, strong hands pulled him backward, and he tumbled to the soft ground.

Again, he was grabbed in friendly hands and dragged away from the fight.

"Lying down on the job, I see," said a familiar voice.

Regdar wiped muck from his eyes and looked up into the face of Captain Gohem Masters. He chuckled and lay back on the mud as, at last, the duke's elite guard rounded the corner and charged into the remaining invaders. Within moments, they overran the black-clad attackers and captured the raft.

Regdar looked up at the ceiling from his cot. He rolled onto his stomach trying to get comfortable but he couldn't—too many wounds. Even after the army's clerics partially cured him, his leg ached, and he still had a painful burn on his face. There weren't enough healing spells to completely cure everyone in one evening.

So the big fighter suffered. He hadn't slept most of the night, despite his exhaustion. Chances were he'd have another sleepless night before the bureaucracy got back around to spreading more healing warmth his way. He rolled onto his back again.

Yep, still hurts, he thought. "Ugh," he moaned, more out of frustration than real pain. "May Pelor see fit to send me a cleric." He rolled to his side. "Any time now," he added.

The sound of heavy boots on the wooden floor of the barrack made Regdar sit up.

He glanced toward the sky. "That was fast."

Light from the early morning sun eased through the door to the chamber, followed by the hulking figure of Duke Christo Ramas. Regdar struggled to rise from bed.

"No, no," said the duke, crossing the room, Captain Masters beside him. "Please rest. There's no need to get up."

Regdar smiled. "Thank you, sir." He relaxed again on his cot. Somehow, it felt more comfortable now.

"It is I who should be thanking you, Captain Regdar." The duke stopped beside his cot. "I'm told that your heroic efforts allowed my guardsmen to get most of the party guests to safety." He reached down and patted Regdar's shoulder. "For that, I am eternally grateful." The duke slid his hands inside his cape and rocked back on his heels. "For your bravery and service to New Koratia, I should be presenting you the Koratian Medal of Honor." He glared down at Regdar. "But instead I'm mad as hell."

Regdar blinked.

"Did you hear nothing I said to you last night?" demanded the duke. "Were my words not sharp enough to pierce that thick skull of yours?"

"I . . . I . . ." stammered Regdar.

"Yes, yes, your actions were brave, blah, blah, blah." The duke pulled his hands from beneath his cape, waving them around in the air. "But you damn near wound up dead." He glanced to the gnome by his side. "I'm informed that if it hadn't been for Captain Masters here and the rest of my elite guard, you'd be resting in a pine box—which I'll tell you is a lot less comfortable than that cot."

Regdar adjusted himself again, looking away from the duke. "I'm not so sure about that."

The duke's eyes narrowed. "Are you trying to get yourself killed, Regdar? Are you really all that wound up over this woman, Naull?"

Regdar jerked his head up in surprise.

The duke smiled. "This old man hears more than you might think," he said, pointing to his own chest with his thumb. Then he knelt down next to Regdar's cot and lowered his voice, talking close to the big fighter's face. "I know what it's like to lose someone close." He nodded and looked around the room. "Every good soldier has lost someone." He took a long, deep breath. "Or worse, been lost by someone."

Regdar nodded, looking away again.

"But we go on," continued the duke. He stood up and raised his voice. "And I expect you to do the same, Captain Regdar." The duke turned and walked toward the door.

Regdar lay back on his cot and looked to the ceiling.

As he crossed the threshold, the duke turned around. "Those soldiers who attacked us, whoever they were," the duke sighed, "I have a feeling we're going to see more of them." He paused. "You were very brave last night, and you should be commended. From today forward, however, you begin acting like an officer. Is that understood?"

Regdar nodded. "Yes, sir."

"Good," replied the duke. Then as he turned to leave he added, "There is an old friend of yours here, someone who I hope will talk some sense into you."

Regdar struggled again to sit up.

The duke smiled. "I'll send him in." He disappeared from sight, followed by Captain Masters.

A moment later, another large frame filled the doorway, back-lit by the rising sun.

"I'm told the hero Regdar could use a cleric," said the man.

"Amen," said the big fighter, lying back once again.

The man crossed the room and looked down on the cot with a big smile on his face, his helm under his arm, and the symbol of Pelor inscribed on his chestplate.

"Jozan!" exclaimed Regdar, jumping slightly. "It's good to see you. I was starting to wonder if I would ever set eyes on you again." Regdar shrugged as he looked down at his bandaged body. "Forgive me if I don't get up and give you a proper greeting."

Jozan chuckled. "Good to see you, too." He knelt down and placed his helm on the floor next to him. "If you think you're getting out of that greeting, think again." Placing one palm on Regdar's forehead and the other on his knee, the cleric prayed softly. "Lord father, grant me the power to release your humble servant from the agony of his wounds. Bind him in your everlasting light and . . ." Jozan's voice trailed off into a low mumble that Regdar couldn't understand.

Then the cleric's hands glowed softly. The light grew, then receded, and Regdar blinked. Little round dots of pale orange floated in his vision, and he wiped his hand across his face. His skin was no longer puckered or scarred, and his leg no longer ached.

"Thank Pelor," he said as he stood at last to embrace his friend.

Jozan rose and returned the welcome.

Breaking away, Regdar hopped a bit on his injured leg, squatting to test it. Satisfied, he headed for the door and motioned Jozan to follow.

"Hungry?" he asked. "The least I can do is buy you a good breakfast while we catch up."

Jozan stayed put. "I'm afraid I don't have time. I'm on urgent business." The cleric took a deep breath. "I'm only passing through briefly."

Regdar stopped and turned around. "Oh." He scratched his head, then stepped back toward the cleric. "Do you need my help?"

Jozan smiled. "Not this time, but thanks for the offer."

Regdar shrugged. "If you didn't come to catch up and you don't need my help, then what did you come to New Koratia for?"

Jozan looked to the ground. "I came—" He hesitated. "I came to tell you about a rumor I heard."

Regdar laughed. "You came all this way to spread gossip?" He stepped up and put his hand on the cleric's forehead. "Maybe it's you who needs healing magic."

Jozan grimaced. "No." He took a deep breath. "I came because I heard word of Naull."

Regdar's eyes narrowed, and he glared at his friend. "Did the duke put you up to this?"

Jozan shook his head. "No, Regdar, he didn't, and I would suspect, judging from what I heard of your conversation, that he wouldn't be happy to know what I'm about to tell you."

Regdar shrugged that away. "What is it then?"

"I've heard that Naull may be alive."

Regdar waved his hands in the air unsteadily. "I saw her disappear into the Elemental Plane of Fire with my own eyes." He turned around and stepped away from the cleric. "She's dead, Jozan. Dead, and I couldn't stop it from happening." Regdar spun on his friend. "Your spreading rumors isn't going to bring her back or—" he gritted his teeth— "make me feel any better about losing her!" He shouted the last word through grinding teeth.

Jozan nodded. "I know, I know, but I'm your friend, Regdar. I wouldn't come to you with news like this unless I were absolutely certain it's reliable."

Regdar blinked. "How do you know this?"

"Two weeks ago, I encountered a group of missionaries who came to the temple for the night. They told me about a slave caravan they encountered—"

"Slave caravan?" Regdar scoffed. "How would missionaries even know a slave from a slave trader? Besides, what are the odds that they'd know Naull?"

Jozan sighed. "That's precisely why I'm here, Regdar." He looked the big fighter in the eye. "One of the men claimed he used to sell apples to an old wizard named Larktiss Dathiendt."

"Naull's mentor?"

"Yes." The cleric nodded. "The same wizard Naull told us stories about when we first met her."

"And this man, this missionary, he'd met Naull before?"

"Referred to her by name, Regdar."

The big fighter scratched his chin. "He has to be mistaken."

"I consulted with Pelor." Jozan pressed his lips together. "Our savior, the god of the sun, gave me a vision—a very strong indication that this rumor is true," persuaded the cleric.

Regdar blinked again. "And you're sure about all this?"

Jozan nodded. "As sure as I am in the power of Pelor that healed your wounds."

Regdar put his forehead in his hand. "You mean she's been alive all this time...." His words slowly trailed off. "If she's alive I should have been looking for her. What must she be enduring right now?" He shook his head and rubbed his temples. "No, no. I saw the City of Fire . . . I saw it disappear . . . This just can't be true." He looked up.

Jozan nodded.

Regdar leaped to his feet. "It doesn't matter. Dead or alive, I've waited too long to find out for myself." He clasped Jozan on the arm. "It will be good to have your company again, my friend."

Jozan grimaced and shook his head. "I can't accompany you, Regdar. As I said, I'm on a quest of my own."

"But I'll need help!"

Jozan cut him off with a stern look. "I'm straining my leave from the church as it is, coming here to tell you what I know."

Regdar took a deep breath and looked around the room. It was empty. He turned his attention back to the cleric.

"I understand."

Jozan reached into his pouch and pulled out a rolled parchment. "This is a map of the Marsh of Haelor, at the base of Mt. Fear."

"To the east?"

"Precisely." Jozan handed the parchment to Regdar. "You will find a mark in the woodlands at the base of the mountain. That is where I believe the caravan was headed."

Regdar took the map and shook his head solemnly. "Thank you, my friend." He clasped Jozan's arm.

The cleric nodded. "I do not know who holds her, Regdar. Be careful, and may Pelor's light guide you when the road becomes dark."

Duke Christo Ramas sat behind his large, cherrywood desk, reading statements from the royal treasury. Two hundred years ago, this very desk belonged to Duke Mikale Ochs, a bloodthirsty tyrant who ruled his duchy with an iron fist. Eventually, his military officers staged a coup, and the duke was stoned to death in the main square of Old Koratia by angry peasants.

Duke Ramas hoped the same fate didn't await him. He dipped his quill in ink and signed a document giving the soldiers a small pay raise.

A knock came at the door to his study.

The duke blew on the fresh ink and put his quill back in its pot. "Enter."

A pasty, hunched-over man in ornate, magenta robes with golden pinstriping came through the door. He bowed.

"Captain Regdar is here to see you."

The duke looked up from his desk. "Regdar, eh. Send him in."

"Very good, my lord." The hunched man bowed again and exited.

A moment later, the door swung open wider, and Regdar stepped across the threshold. He dropped to one knee.

"Rise, Captain," said the duke, standing behind his desk. "Come in."

Regdar stood up, closed the heavy wooden door behind him, and stepped farther into the room.

"I suspect your conversation with the good cleric went well."

"Yes, sir, it did."

The duke smiled. "And I also suspect you've come to tell me he talked some sense into that fool head of yours." He chuckled.

"Not exactly, sir," replied the big fighter.

The duke stopped laughing.

Regdar puffed himself up to his full height and stood at perfect attention. "I've come to resign my commission, sir."

Duke Ramas strode around his desk and leaned back against its front edge. "Now, son, I realize I was a little hard on you today, but—"

"No, sir," interrupted Regdar. "I believe you were entirely fair and honest with me."

The duke shook his head, confused. "Then what is this all about?"

Regdar glanced down, looking uncomfortable. "It's about Naull, sir. I believe she's still alive."

Duke Ramas pinched the bridge of his nose. "And you wish to resign your commission so you can go find her, is that it?"

"Yes, sir."

The duke pounded his fist on the desk. "And what am I supposed to do when these black-armored soldiers come marching on New Koratia again? I need you here, Regdar, now more than ever."

Regdar nodded.

The duke was frustrated. "These things I've been saying to you, these talks we've been having aren't just about you being more careful, they're about you learning how to take larger responsibility."

"Yes, sir, I know," replied Regdar. "Now I have a responsibility to myself to find out if the woman I love is still alive." He stepped closer to the duke. "This is something I have to do. You have plenty of capable soldiers who can defend New Koratia while I'm gone, and when I return—"

"Your duty is to this duchy, Captain Regdar," interrupted the duke, standing up to his full height and stepping up to look the big fighter in the eye. "If you leave now, don't ever show your face in my territory again, or you will be hanged from a gallows for abandoning your post. Do I make myself clear?"

Regdar gritted his teeth. "Perfectly." He unhitched his shield from his back. He looked at the red dragon crest—the field arms of the New Koratian military—on its front, then let it fall to the ground.

The duke flinched as it crashed to the hard wood floor.

Regdar saluted, turned on his heals, and exited the room, quietly shutting the door behind him.

The duke rubbed his eyes with his calloused palm. He sighed.

"May Pelor light your way, young man. May Pelor light your way."

In the dying evening light, Regdar paced outside the barrack door. What would he tell the men? If Naull was being held by slavers, then one fighter, no matter how strong, wasn't going to be able to rescue her. He needed their help but he was no longer their captain. He took a deep breath, steadied himself, and marched toward the open door.

Regdar crossed through the first chamber and into the bunk room. Whitman, Tasca, Clemf, and Krunk all looked up from their cots. He looked back.

"Well?" prompted Whitman after a pregnant pause.

Regdar paced the room, thinking about what he was going to say. He stopped and faced the four men, forcing a smile.

"The duke has given us his blessing," he said, nodding.

"Even after what happened last night?" asked Tasca.

Regdar stood to his full height. "The duke has confidence that the New Koratian military and his elite guards can handle the situation, with or without our help."

Tasca shrugged. "Okay then, what are we waiting for? Let's go find your woman."

The men began hefting their already-packed backpacks.

Regdar coughed into his fist.

The men stopped.

"I must remind you that this mission, like many in the past, is undertaken on a volunteer-only basis." He looked each of them in the eye. "You are under no obligation to go."

They all laughed, shouldering their gear and heading past Regdar out the door.

The big fighter smiled, grabbed his own belongings, and fell into step behind Clemf at the end of the line.

The party marched through the gates and down the River Delnir toward the Southern Sea. The moon slowly rose in the darkening sky, and the sound of crickets and the running river filled the soldiers' ears.

"Nice night," said Tasca.

"Only an elf would say that," jabbed Whitman.

"What is that supposed to mean?"

"Oh, I don't know," replied the dwarf, "maybe you ought to write us some poetry about the moonlight and the romantic crickets. Maybe the pretty little elf boy should have been a bard."

Tasca pulled his rapier from his belt, flipped it endwise, and conked the dwarf on the helm with the bell. The heavy dwarven helmet rang loud in the quiet night, and the crickets stopped chirping.

"Will you two knock it off?" scolded Regdar. "Thanks to you all the bears and bandits know we're out here."

"It's better that way," said Whitman, smiling as he readjusted his helm. "I prefer a straight fight to all this sneaking around."

"Duck!" Clemf landed hard on Regdar's back, and the two men hit the ground.

"What the—" Regdar rolled over, ready to curse Clemf for his clumsiness, but found himself staring up at a river troll.

Whitman tumbled into action. Rolling forward, he came up at the foot of the beast. The shiny, dwarven-worked head of his weapon crashed down with a tremendous thud and a crack.

The troll's thigh bone visibly collapsed, and its knee shot out at an odd angle. The creature hissed at the dwarf and swung back. Its claws raked along the side of Whitman's helm. The spine-tingling screech, like the sound of a razor scraping soft stone, made Regdar cringe.

The dwarf, however, seemed not to mind. "That the best you got, you slimy giant?" cursed Whitman.

Tasca winked at Krunk before jumping into combat and slicing his blade across the troll's arm.

A long gash opened up, and dark green fluid poured out, dripping to the ground and splashing on Whitman.

"Damn you, elf," shouted the stout, little man.

"You should be taller," replied Tasca, dodging the troll's backhand.

A second troll pulled itself from the banks of the river. The mottled green beast dived into the fray, but Clemf and Krunk intercepted it before it could reach its companion.

"Must be a female," shouted Krunk, ducking under a clawed fist.

Clemf lunged forward, jabbing his longsword at the green giant. "How do you know?"

Krunk's mace connected with a meaty slap, ripping away a large hunk of flesh. "Because it's bigger than the other."

Regdar shook off his pack and clambered to his feet, then circled behind the first troll. The slash on its arm had already stopped bleeding, and the skin was closing over. Its leg, too, was straightening, but Whitman's heavy blow had shattered the bone so that even the rapidly recovering beast moved slower than normal.

While Tasca and Whitman kept the monster at bay, Regdar rushed in from behind it. The troll saw its danger and tried to squirm away at the last minute, but being pinned between three opponents, it had nowhere to go. Regdar's greatsword cleaved deeply into the rubbery hide.

More green blood flooded to the ground, once again splashing Whitman. The troll staggered around and glared down at Regdar.

"What's this?" Tasca leered at Whitman. "No criticism for Regdar?" He lunged in and his blade skipped from the beast's heavy hide.

"Why would I?" replied the dwarf, bringing his hammer down on the troll's foot. "This is all your fault."

Tasca stumbled back from the troll's backswing and landed on his seat. "Of course," he said, lifting himself from the ground and sneering at the dwarf. "I almost forgot."

The troll limped a half-step forward and swung at Regdar. The claws on its mighty right hand connected with the fighter's ribcage, producing a loud, cracking sound. The blow knocked the air from Regdar's lungs. The creature's second claw swung down, to catch the big fighter on the thigh. Its digits wrapped around Regdar's leg as if it were a chicken wing, then the troll leaned back and yanked. Regdar dropped his sword in the struggle to free himself from the monster's grip. It was no use. The troll had him tight, and the big fighter's flesh tore under the troll's rending claws.

Regdar howled in pain. The monster's claws made a popping

sound as they pulled out of his side, then scraped across the metal of his armor. The big fighter fell to the ground, shaken and bleeding. The stretched, ripped skin between his ribs and leg felt as if it were on fire.

The troll seemed quite pleased with itself.

Braced on his hands and knees, Regdar spit on the ground. A long, thin line of red trailed through the center of the viscous saliva, and he growled.

Regdar picked up his sword and got to his feet as quickly as he could manage. "I've had about enough of you," he shouted. Then he stepped forward, covering almost his full height in a single step, and aimed a powerful blow at the troll.

The sudden attack surprised the monster. Regdar's blade bit deep into the troll's side, forcing it to hop back on its broken leg. That brought it nearly atop Whitman, who smashed his hammer against the creature's back. Tasca's rapier flashed in the moonlight. It glanced off the creature's shoulder before spearing deep into its neck.

The troll roared and shook its head. Tasca's blade came free of his hand, its point still stuck in the side of the giant's throat. The monster clawed at its neck and chest, gouging the flesh with its nails.

A huge flash lit the dark sky. Over Whitman's shoulder, the second troll burst into flames. Beside the beast stood Clemf holding a broken glass bottle in his hand. Krunk crouched next to him, his hand in the air, a small, magical flame in his palm.

Regdar had no time to ask what they'd done. The troll before him, despite its horrid wounds, managed to dislodge Tasca's rapier and toss it to the ground as if it were a toothpick. The beast flailed its arms in a frenzy, nearly catching Whitman in the chest and sending Tasca sprawling out of the way. Regdar ducked under a poorly aimed blow and stepped inside the creature's reach.

With a well-placed jab, the big fighter rammed his sword into the soft flesh between the creature's ribs. Dropping to one knee, Regdar lowered his shoulder and put all of his strength behind an upward thrust. His blade disappeared up to its hilt inside the creature's chest, devoured entirely by slick, green flesh.

The troll's arms fell to its sides, and it raised its head to the sky. A stinking, fang-lined mouth opened wide, as if it were cursing whatever god a troll might worship or despise. With a tremendous shudder, the giant leaned forward and vomited on Regdar. Dark green bile, punctuated with shiny, black gobs, rained over the fighter.

Finally spent, the monster toppled back and landed with a thud on the hard ground.

Regdar stood motionless, his hands out at his sides, breathing from his open mouth. His sword jutted at an angle from the fallen creature's chest. Behind it, Krunk and Clemf danced around the second, flaming troll. The little dwarf threw fistfuls of fire at the burning monster while the human splashed it with lamp oil. Both bobbed and weaved, staying out of reach of the very angry creature that was thankfully blinded by the flames and the pain.

Regdar felt a hand resting on his shoulder.

"You okay, chief?" Whitman asked.

Regdar shook himself back to reality and focused on the slowly healing wound in the troll's ribs where it was transfixed by his sword. His lip curled in disgust.

"Never better," he spat. Stepping forward, the fighter grabbed his sword and sawed it sideways through the troll's body. More green liquid spilled out.

Regdar ignored it.

Lifting his sword over his head, Regdar sliced it across the monster's neck. The blade cut through rubbery flesh and found the cartilage between two vertebrae before hitting the hard-packed dirt. The troll's head rolled free, flopped awkwardly as it rotated once, twice, then came to a stop, nose in the air. The body convulsed.

"That's one way to do it," commented Tasca, looking down at the dead giant.

"Indeed," agreed Whitman.

A loud screech brought Regdar's attention to the other troll. Its flesh bubbled and cracked in the flames. Dark smoke rose toward the sky, and a heavy stench, like burning feces, filled the air. Flames encased every inch of the beast, making it look like a fire elemental.

Squawking out its pain, the troll collapsed to its knees. It flopped onto its face, and its burning hand came to rest on the other troll's decapitated head. Then it finally stopped moving, and the whole mass continued to burn.

Regdar sat back on his heels. "I don't know about any of you, but I vote we find a place with flowing water and no trolls and camp for the night."

Regdar hissed as he lifted his chestplate from his shoulders. He let it fall to the dirt with a loud crash. His tattered and torn undershirt was stained crimson in a long oval from his shoulder to his belly and all down his torso. He lifted the ruined garment gingerly from his body and tossed it into the slowly growing fire Whitman tended.

Regdar examined himself. Along his left side, three large puncture wounds weeped a clear, yellow liquid, dotted with flecks of dark red. Jagged pink stretch marks ran across his body from his ribs, past his belly button, and down onto his right hip. He poked at them with his finger and drew in air between gritted teeth. The scratches burned. The pain wasn't as bad as when the troll made them, but they burned nonetheless.

Sitting down on a mossy stump, Regdar doffed the rest of his armor. His right thigh had a huge bruise from hip to knee, but it was otherwise intact. The fighter sighed. He was glad most of the injuries were superficial. Bruises hurt but would heal, and he could fight without too much trouble. His ribs, however, were a different story.

"Let me look at that." Krunk pointed at the holes in Regdar's side with his stubby fingers.

"Be my guest." With considerable effort, Regdar lifted his arm and twisted to his right.

"Hmm." Krunk scratched at his long, white beard.

"How is it?"

The hair on the front of the dwarf's face moved. Regdar assumed Krunk was either smiling or cringing.

"Well, it's not diseased," replied the dwarf.

Tasca coughed out a laugh from the other side of the fire. "That the best you could come up with? Your words inspire confidence in us all."

Whitman elbowed him in the ribs. "Shut up, elf."

Krunk's moustache moved again. "I think I can patch you up good as new," he said. Reaching into his tunic, he pulled out a finely crafted cross with the symbol of the sun emblazoned on it. The cross was made from what looked in the flickering firelight like silver or platinum, and the reaching bands of the holy sun were obviously gold.

Wrapping the thick fingers of one hand around the religious artifact, Krunk placed his other palm on Regdar's chest above the weeping wounds. The dwarf closed his eyes and recited a prayer under his breath.

Regdar felt Krunk's fingers tighten on his skin, then the familiar, healing warmth flowed into his frame. He leaned his head back and rolled his eyes deeper into their sockets. He loved this sensation. It was almost worth getting hurt just to be healed again.

Lost in the warm relief provided by Krunk's spell, Regdar flinched when something touched his leg. Lifting his head, he looked down to see the dwarf cleric preparing to heal the bruise there.

"You should try to not get hurt so much." Krunk pushed on the soft, purple tissue on the big fighter's leg.

Regdar squirmed and gritted his teeth. The euphoria from the previous healing spell was all but gone.

"One of these days," Krunk continued, "I might not be around to fix you up, and then where will you be?" He pressed his palm again into the fighter's flesh and mouthed a few short words.

Regdar felt the healing warmth again, though much weaker. He moved his left arm and squeezed his thigh. Both felt better.

"Thanks, Krunk," he said, standing up from the stump and walking to his pack. "I owe you one."

The old dwarf stomped to the fire and sat next to Clemf. "Don't start counting now," he said. "You never have before, and you'll never be rich enough to pay your debts anyway."

They all laughed.

Regdar drew a new shirt over his shoulders. "You're probably right about that." Then he, too, sat by the fire.

Tasca and Clemf held long, carved tree branches over the fire. On the end of them, each man had a row of punctured mushrooms roasting above the flames.

Whitman pulled a package wrapped in a handkerchief from his pack and returned to the fire. He lifted the cloth and began tearing off large hunks of bread and handing them around. Tasca pulled his mushrooms from the flames and pointed the stick at Regdar, who used his hunk of bread to pull a bubbling fungus from the branch.

"Thanks," he said, putting the impromptu sandwich to his lips and blowing on the hot meal.

Whitman did the same. "So," he said between cooling breaths, "you really think we'll be able to find this woman?"

Regdar looked up over his mushroom. "I wouldn't have asked you to come here if I didn't."

"How did you lose her in the first place?" asked Tasca.

Whitman elbowed Tasca again.

Regdar raised his hand. "It's all right, Whitman. Telling you the story is the least I can do."

The other men looked up, and Regdar began.

"Have any of you ever heard of the City of Fire?"

"The mythical City of Fire?" asked Krunk.

Regdar nodded. "I thought it mythical too until I walked its streets."

Whitman scratched his beard. "So it really exists?"

"Well, it did." Regdar sighed. "I and my companions sent it back to the planes." Regdar stopped for a minute, rubbed his face, and swallowed away the tightness in his throat. "We were fighting a crazed blackguard who wanted a powerful artifact from inside the city. She almost got it, too, but Naull managed to trap her inside a magic bubble." He looked up into the night sky. "It worked great, except that Naull was trapped inside the sphere as well. To keep the artifact out of the hands of evil, we sent the city back through its planar gate." He paused. "Naull was still trapped inside."

Everyone sat silent, not even chewing their food.

Clemf was the first to break the silence. "You watched her go?"

Regdar closed his eyes and nodded.

"And you assumed she was dead," added Tasca.

Regdar shrugged. "The city went to the Elemental Plane of Fire. Once her spell ended, there was no way she could survive there."

"And this cleric friend of yours, Jozan," said Whitman, "he had proof that she's still alive."

Regdar nodded. "Proof enough to persuade him. I know what you're all thinking, but if there's even a chance that she didn't die in that fire, then I have to find out for myself." He looked at them all in turn. "Like I said back in the barrack, this is a volunteer mission. You're under no obligation to stay."

There was a moment of silence, cut only by the sound of the crackling flames.

"Well, I don't know about the rest of you," said Tasca, "but I was sold when he told me we were going to rescue a kidnapped woman from a band of slavers." The elf pulled another mushroom off his branch. "I have a terrible weakness for damsels in distress."

Whitman glared at the elf. "We're with you, Regdar."

The others nodded.

Regdar smiled. "I know. I know."

Krunk was awakened by Tasca when the moon was high overhead.

"Your turn," said the elf before he climbed into his bedroll.

Krunk rolled to his feet and wiped the sleep from his eyes. The others were fast asleep.

The fire burned low in the pit Whitman had made. Tasca had been smart to keep it small. There was no point in attracting more attention than necessary.

Picking up his mace, Krunk walked around the fire. A small pile of branches rested nearby. Krunk smiled. Despite what Whitman said about him, Tasca was an upstanding fellow.

Krunk sat for a while, poking at the fire with a long stick, throwing another branch on when the flames grew too weak.

The night passed slowly, stars moving imperceptibly across the sky. The dwarf became sleepy again. Shaking his head, Krunk got to his feet and went to collect more wood for the fire.

Before trudging to the riverbank, the cleric hung his mace from his belt. It was mid-summer, and the waters of the River Delnir were low. Spring runoff had deposited plenty of firewood high on the banks, and Krunk quickly made a heaping pile to carry back.

"That should last till morning," he said as he bent down to pick up the wood.

Something that felt like two huge rocks hit him on the back.

His face crashed into the pile of branches, and he was pinned to the ground. The air was driven from his lungs.

Krunk twisted as hard as he could to right and left, but he was stuck. Whatever was on top of him was either larger or stronger than he, or both. He heard a crackle and a pop, like a bone being separated from its joint. A burst of warm, damp air rushed across the back of his neck, setting all the tiny hairs on end.

The dwarf cleric could hear his heart beat in his ears. His thoughts raced. The smell of rotting flesh reached his nose, and a sharp pain ran down his spine. In a flash he understood.

Vampire.

Regdar awoke with a start, his hand instinctively wrapped around his greatsword. He shook his head and sat up. The others were sleeping, and the fire had all but gone out. A smoking pile of dull, red embers was all that remained.

"Krunk," he said in a loud whisper.

Only the sound of the running river, several paces away, answered back.

"Krunk," he said again, a little louder this time.

In the low glow of the embers, Regdar could see Whitman sit up straight, clutching his hammer to his chest.

Regdar got to his feet and crossed to the dwarf. Without a word, Whitman reached over and shook Tasca awake, laying his finger across his lips, signaling silence. The elf got the hint and lifted himself from his sleeping roll while retrieving his rapier.

Regdar turned to wake Clemf.

A heavy, wooden club swung through the air, just missing his head. The big fighter stumbled back and let out a shout, surprised by the attack. In front of him, hunched over the sleeping form of Clemf, stood a ghastly black and green monstrosity.

The creature's body was covered in rippled scales, and the back of its neck sported something like a fish's fin. Though it looked like a giant lizard with a long, winding tongue, it stood erect like a man. In one hand it held the club that had almost crushed Regdar's head. In the other it carried a large shield.

At first, Regdar thought the creature's eyes were reflecting the dull glow of the fire. Then he realized they were burning a fiery red all their own. The monster, whatever it was, opened its mouth and let out a whooshing hiss. Its teeth were long and jagged, but what impressed Regdar the most were the fangs that protruded from the thing's upper and lower jaws. Four in all, and each looked as long and sharp as Tasca's rapier.

Clemf, still curled under his blanket, rolled over and continued sleeping while the monster crouched above him.

Circling to one side, Regdar moved away from the fire, trying his best to get behind the thing. His ploy worked, because the creature spun and moved away from Clemf.

"That's a good little lizard vampire thing," said Regdar, wishing he had gone to sleep in his armor. "Come and get it."

As if responding to the big fighter's taunt, the lizard creature leaped at him. It moved with surprising speed and grace, its tail slithering along the ground behind it. Regdar dodged back, fighting defensively, keeping anything he might not want bitten off as far away from the creature's mouth as possible.

The greatclub swiped in at waist level. Regdar bashed it away. A claw slashed out of nowhere from the other side. Regdar sidestepped it. Teeth snapped shut before his face, moonlight glinting from the long, sharp fangs. Regdar almost gagged on the foul stench of rotting flesh. He stumbled back again.

The creature paced forward, letting out another hiss.

"Foul beast," hollered Whitman. His hammer was poised for a blow.

The lizard creature reacted quickly and swung its tail at the stout dwarf. Whitman tried to jump clear, but the scaly appendage hit him in the feet. He tumbled across the ground and down the river embankment.

Regdar lunged forward, taking advantage of the distraction. His blade caught the creature below the jaw, opening a wound along its neck. Black ooze dribbled out, and the beast's attention returned to the human fighter. It waggled its long, gray tongue, slopping foul-smelling liquid all over the ground and on Regdar's sword.

The creature hissed, then spun around in time to catch Tasca's rapier on its shield. The blade made a hollow thump as it hit, and the tip stuck in the soft material. Leaping into the air, the elf kicked out with both feet against the lizard thing's shield, one on each side of his lodged sword. The impact forced the creature back a step, and Tasca fell to the ground, his sword once again in his hand.

Regdar stepped in again, taking a mighty swing at the vampire's tail. He connected with a crash. A heavy scale broke into bits and scattered in the moonlight. Regdar was rewarded with a heavy thump to the chest as the tail flicked back. It knocked the wind from his lungs and the man from his feet.

Landing hard on his back, Regdar tried to inhale. He couldn't. It was as if the air around him had been sucked away. Time slowed down, and everything he did, even blinking his eyes, felt labored and difficult. He stared up into the dark sky. The moon seemed so big among the tiny stars. His head felt like a watermelon, and the skin on his face felt hot and red.

Then something moved into his field of view, something larger even than the moon. Clutching his sword in his right hand, the big fighter looked up into the gaping maw of the vampire lizard. Its red eyes burned as they looked down on him. It growled, a sound that filled the surrounding space, drowning out all other noise—the wind, the crickets, even the rushing river.

The monster leaned forward to glare down at him, and a gob of

thick, black liquid splashed across Regdar's face. The lizard creature flew out of his view, and a huge forearm emblazoned with the
image of a longsword came in, followed immediately by Clemf's
tightly gritted face. Then it too disappeared.

Regdar gasped again, this time with limited success. Sound
returned to his ears. He heard the burbling river and the sucking
noise of Clemf's sword plunging into monster's flesh. Rolling to
his side, the fighter struggled to his feet.

Tasca and Clemf battled the monster from either side. The elf
teased scales from its body with his dancing blade. The enormous
human bashed large chunks of flesh from its hide. Somehow the
creature had lost or discarded its club and shield. Spinning first
one way, then back, the vampire swiped with its claws. It hissed at
both men but was unable to focus on one without opening itself
to a deadly assault from the other.

The standoff was broken when a hurtling, twisting mass of
dwarf and hammer flew over the riverbank and plunged on top of
the vampiric lizard.

Whitman's hammer crashed into the monster's reptilian head,
making a hollow sound like a mallet on a coconut. The creature's
skull ruptured. Chunks of yellow curd shot out in a wave. The
resulting splash covered the head of the dwarf's weapon with dripping ooze.

The vampire collapsed to the ground.

"Agh!" shouted Whitman as he landed. "Brain juice! Vampire
lizardman brain juice on my hammer."

Regdar opened his mouth, then shut it again. He was sure there
was something worse in this world to get on your hammer, but he
couldn't think of it at the moment.

Tasca and Clemf stepped back from the slumped monster, looking quickly in all directions to be sure the area was clear. Regdar
checked to the riverbank.

"Anybody see Krunk?" he asked.

"No," said Whitman, now on his knees feverishly rubbing dirt on his hammer.

"No," replied Clemf.

"Over there!" Tasca broke into a run, pointing at something with his sword.

Regdar and Clemf followed.

Just at the edge of the embankment, where the plain sloped down toward the River Delnir, lay Krunk. He was facedown and spread-eagle atop a pile of branches.

Regdar crouched beside him. Blood covered most of the back of his head, neck, and shoulders, brimming from a savage wound where the monster had bitten nearly through his neck. His arms and most of his face were scratched and cut.

"He put up a fight," said Regdar.

"Wouldn't you?" asked Tasca.

Regdar shrugged, feeling a bit stupid.

Clemf kicked the dirt. "It had to be the cleric," he said.

Tasca looked up, shaking his head. "What are you talking about? It could have been any of us."

Clemf stowed his sword and raised his hands in the air. "Yeah, it could have, but it was the cleric."

Tasca slumped as he realized what Clemf meant.

"There's only one thing we can do," Regdar said.

He stood. Lifting his sword over his head, he brought it down with a heavy grunt. The blade sliced through the bloody remains of Krunk's neck, and the dwarf's head rolled free.

Tasca jumped back. "Are you mad?" he screamed. "He was our friend."

Clemf, too, looked uneasy.

Regdar grabbed the dismembered head by the beard. "He was, but he wouldn't be when he rose from the dead. Help me with his body," he said.

The others looked on, horrified.

Regdar stood up and looked at the elf and the human, Krunk's head still dangling from his hand.

"He was bitten by a vampire," he explained. "If we simply bury him, he'll come back as a vampire." He looked the other two men in the eyes. "Something tells me a holy man such as Krunk here—" he lifted the upside-down head, its eyes peering out lifelessly at the others— "would rather not return to the world as an undead monster." He turned and headed down the embankment. "Now, if you really were Krunk's friends, you'll help me bury him in the river, so he can ascend in the afterlife, or whatever it is dwarves do when they die."

The next two days were silent and uneventful. If not for the family of rabbits Tasca shot for dinner the second night, the rest of the journey to the base of Mt. Fear would have been completely forgettable. As it turned out, the elf knew a thing or two about finding wild herbs and roasting fresh game. Dinner that night was delicious.

Late morning of the third day brought the party to the wooded area marked on Jozan's map. The looming, jagged top of Mt. Fear towered above the plain. As the sun rose higher in the sky, the circle of clouds lingering around its peak slowly dissipated, showing off the deep chasm between the two wicked points that distinguished this mountain from all others in the land.

At its base, a dense growth of trees formed a ring around the mountain. Unlike other forests, this one grew up out of a fetid, rotting swamp. Tangled brambles intermingled with algae and pools of rotting vegetation. The tree roots didn't plunge into rich, fertile soil to pucker the ground in long, oval mounds. Instead, they reached out like hungry fingers, groping into the graying filth of the swamp, looking like thick, chaotic spiderwebs as they crisscrossed each other in search of food.

Regdar stopped the men at the edge of this sloppy ring.

"Jozan said we'd find the slavers inside this, the Marsh of Haelor." He put his hands on his hips and looked at the dense growth. "If I were evil, I'd definitely find this place homey."

Tasca stepped up beside the fighter. "Listen, Regdar, I know what you say your cleric pal told you, but something doesn't make sense here."

Regdar turned to the elf. "Yeah, Naull's in there—" He pointed to the swamp— "and we're out here."

Tasca nodded while biting his lower lip. "That too." The edges of his lips curled up into an amused smile. "But I meant that if the guys we're looking for are slavers, why would they set up camp in a swamp?" The elf wrinkled his brow. "Not exactly a prime location to do business."

"He's right." Whitman ran his fingers through his long beard. "I've seen slaver caravans. They travel the same routes as the carnivals, and they're not the type to set up camp anywhere for more than a night, maybe two at the most. They're constantly on the go—not real popular in areas where they capture their slaves. But they need people to kidnap and people to sell to. Why would they hole up in forsaken spot like this?"

Regdar nodded. "Remote as it is, this region is still under the protection of Duke Ramas. He's not a man who tolerates slavers. Maybe they're just taking a rest in a place they consider secure."

"Could the cleric have made a mistake?" asked Tasca.

Regdar remained grim. "It wouldn't be the first time. Still, he said he'd been given signs from Pelor." He shrugged. "The god of the sun works in strange ways. It's possible Jozan misunderstood the details but not the intent. Where Pelor's concerned, Jozan knows what he's talking about." The big fighter turned away from his friends and continued walking. "Whatever the case, I'm not going back until I find Naull or I'm convinced she's not here."

The others fell in behind him, skirting the edge of the wooded area, looking for a passable entrance into the tangled swamp.

Whitman sniffed the air. "It reeks."

"That's your upper lip," quipped Tasca.

"Swamp gas," corrected Regdar. He stopped again, peering into the interior. "How do you suppose they got in? The four of us could step tree root to tree root I suppose, but a larger group, especially one with an unwilling hostage, would want a more stable path."

"Maybe Naull went willingly," said Clemf.

Regdar turned and grabbed Clemf by his chestplate, shaking the man.

"Hey now," complained Clemf. "I'm just saying . . . Let's consider all the possibilities."

Regdar glared for a moment longer, then let him go. "It's not a possibility." His frustration was near the boiling point. The woman he loved might still be alive and captive. He wanted to smash something, kill those who held her hostage, punish whoever kept her from him.

But he couldn't.

He couldn't do anything except look for a needle in a haystack.

But Clemf was right. Regdar wasn't certain of anything, least of all whether Naull was even alive, and his frustration was starting to wear at the edges.

Tasca broke the silence, interrupting the tense moment. "There, just under those hanging vines." The elf pointed to a solid-looking dirt path in the dark interior of the forest, just beyond a large, murky field of water.

Clemf turned away, and Regdar looked to where Tasca pointed.

"I see it," replied the big fighter. "But they'd have to cross the water. Do you think it's shallow enough?"

"There's only one way to find out," replied the elf.

"Yes," interjected Whitman, "but what do you think lives in water like that?"

"Eels," replied Clemf. "Big ones."

Regdar turned to the tattooed human. "Why would you say that?"

Clemf pointed to the water near the far edge.

Regdar turned back. Sure enough, he saw a giant ripple move through the water, pushing away the scum in an **S** shape.

Whitman was already pulling a coil of rope from his pack. "I'll go first," he said matter-of-factly. "You boys tie off. If one of us falls in, the others can pull him out."

"What if a giant eel gets one of us?" asked Tasca.

"Don't worry," said Whitman with a smile. "If elf flesh tastes as bad as it smells, the eel will spit you back out again." He chuckled as he finished tying the end of the rope around his waist. "Or it'll gag you back up."

Tasca shrugged his shoulders. "He might seem offensive if he weren't short enough to fit inside my boot."

"I'm not short," bellowed the dwarf, wading into the grimy water.

Tasca tied off behind Clemf, third in line. "Gets him every time." He laughed and followed the tattooed man into the swamp.

Regdar put his hand on Clemf's shoulder.

"I'm—" started Regdar.

Clemf cut him off with a wave of his hand. "Don't worry," he said. "I'd be the same way if my lady were in trouble." He gripped his friend's arm, then waded into the swamp.

Regdar took up the rear, his left hand firmly on the rope around his waist, his right gripping the hilt of his greatsword.

The water was cold, and the muck floating on top smelled like rotten goblin flesh. The bottom of the swamp was squishy, and it made forward movement quite hard. Still, despite the difficulties, the water came up only to the top of Regdar's thigh (right below Whitman's chest), and it seemed the swamp was passable after all.

Whitman made it out the other side and onto dry land without a problem. Clemf followed, then Tasca.

Regdar could feel the bottom sloping upward under his feet when something brushed the back of his leg.

Tasca opened his mouth. Regdar listened to hear what his friend had to say. It sounded like water rushing past his ears. Then Tasca's face disappeared. What was going on? he thought. Fetid swamp water rushed inside his armor, bringing with it the cold and the realization that his feet had been pulled forward from under him.

Landing on his back on the squishy bottom, Regdar looked up into blurry blackness. He reflexively tried to breathe, but the thick water quickly cut off that urge. He had swallowed some through his nose on the way down, and a burning sensation now ran down his nostrils and along the back of his throat. He managed to keep hold of his sword, but it wasn't doing him any good down here.

The creature, presumably an eel, was wrapped around his legs. It continually tightened and loosened its grip. The sensation of being squeezed then released then squeezed again was unsettling, and Regdar struggled against it.

Something squeezed him around his waist. This one was skinnier than whatever trapped his legs, but it pulled with such insistent strength that it lifted him off the bottom. The eel around his legs pulled to his right, and Regdar spun sideways.

Great, he thought, they're fighting over me.

Maneuvering his greatsword as best he could, Regdar twisted the blade and drew it across the eel's flesh. The creature's rubbery hide was tough, however, and the blade's edge slipped right off. The attack apparently angered the beast.

Regdar was yanked through the water. His head breached the surface, and his chest came up into the air. He coughed out a mouthful of foul water as he toppled over. The serpent at his feet pulled him back toward deeper water while the one around his waist pulled him forward.

Shaking the water from his face, Regdar opened his eyes in time to watch the muddy ground come up to greet him. He landed on his chest with a dull thud and a grunt. Immediately, the serpent around his legs strained to pull him back into the water.

"Pull," yelled Clemf.

Regdar looked up.

The human, the elf, and the dwarf leaned back hard on the rope attached to their waists.

Regdar looked down.

The serpent around his middle wasn't a serpent at all but a rope, now with a huge gash where he'd attacked it.

Rolling over, Regdar saw the shiny, black hide of a giant eel wrapped firmly around his legs just above his ankles. He pulled his knees to his chest and swung his sword at his feet. The magical weapon connected with serpent scales and bit deep. A gush of purplish blue blood ran onto the muddy bank.

The pulling at his waist stopped, and Clemf's huge arms wrapped around Regdar's shoulders. To his right, Whitman tumbled into view, coming up on his feet and landing a hammer blow to the back of the serpent. Tasca appeared to the left, cutting into the wound Regdar had inflicted and slicing almost all the way through the creature's body.

The eel recoiled at the assault and loosened its grip on Regdar's legs. Uncoiling, the creature's body slithered over the prone fighter, spinning around and around in a circle like the chains unwinding from a drawbridge. Finally, a pointed tail flashed through the air, and the giant eel swam off into the murky water.

Regdar relaxed his shoulders and dropped back into the mud.

"Are you all right?" Whitman stared him first in one eye, then the other.

Regdar coughed up a bit of thick, black water that dribbled

from his lips. "Never better," he said with a burp. Then he rolled over and vomited.

After he finished emptying his stomach, Clemf lifted him to his feet.

"Someone's approaching," murmured Tasca in a loud whisper.

Whitman tumbled into the heavy brush beside the path.

Clemf grabbed Regdar by the back of the arm and shoved him behind a large tree.

Tasca crouched down into a squat, then jumped into the air. He caught a branch nearly three times his height off the ground. Then, swinging his feet, he lifted himself into the canopy of the tree, out of sight.

Not more than a heartbeat later, three black-clad soldiers, all wearing the same spiked scale mail as the men who attacked Duke Ramas's keep, entered the swamp from the plain, following the same path Regdar and his companions had used. Though it had been difficult for Regdar, these men made it look easy, as if they had done it many times before and had no fear of the giant eels.

They passed the hidden comrades without any indication of noticing them.

An arrow sailed out of the treetops and nailed one of the soldiers in the neck, dropping him to his knees.

Whitman somersaulted from the brush, back-flipping to a stop before the stunned soldiers. His hammer barred their path.

Clemf stepped from behind the tree, longsword leveled, blocking their escape back through the swamp.

Regdar stepped into clear view, his ornate longbow pulled taught, an arrow nocked and pointed at the trapped men.

"We can do this the easy way," Regdar chuckled, "or you can make it hard on yourselves."

The black-clad soldiers stood completely still.

"We've come looking for a woman," said Regdar, moving a bit closer. "A wizard named Naull."

The two soldiers still on their feet turned to glare at Regdar with malice in their eyes.

The man on his knees pulled his helm from his head. Tasca's arrow was lodged in the side of his neck, and the wound bled freely. Regdar could see that he would bleed to death before long without aid. The wounded man threw his helmet at Whitman and drew his sword, still on his knees.

"I thought so," said Regdar through gritted teeth. He let his arrow fly. It connected with the kneeling man's ear, knocking him stiffly sideways and pinning his head to the ground.

The other two men drew their swords, then both lunged forward at Whitman. The dwarf bashed away one attack but suffered a cut to the shoulder from the other. Reversing the head of his hammer, he used the momentum from his swing to wind up for another attack. The head of his dwarven-forged weapon collided with a bone-splitting crack against one man's shins. The soldier dropped to a crouch, clutching his obviously broken leg.

Clemf rammed his longsword into the back of the other man's ribcage. The scale mail separated before the sharp point, and the man gasped, arching his spine. The man stumbled away from Clemf's blade on his toes. He ran blindly into Whitman, who refused to give ground.

With a half step forward, Clemf held the man pinned on the end of his blade like a giant bug.

"Drop your sword," he growled, "or I'll saw this blade right down through your guts."

Regdar nocked another arrow. "You've heard of the woman Naull?"

The two black-clad soldiers remained still.

Regdar stepped up and kicked the soldier's broken shin.

The man collapese to his side, whimpering. His face wrinkled up, and the ridges faded into white as he clinched against the pain.

Clemf twisted his sword, the tip still lodged in the other soldier's back. The man moaned and gripped the hilt of his own sword tighter. Whitman nudged him with his shoulder, pushing him farther onto Clemf's blade.

Regdar kicked the downed man again. "I'm going to keep asking you until you tell me," he said, exaggerating each word and pausing after each one to land another kick.

The standing soldier inhaled deeply, with much pain. Then he lurched forward and slashed with his sword toward Whitman. It was a stroke of defiance—he hadn't the strength remaining to be truly dangerous.

In a blink, however, four men moved.

An arrow launched down from the treetop, slicing into the back of the man's neck, missing the helm entirely and sinking into the soft flesh below the head.

Clemf lunged forward, twisting his blade with all of his considerable strength.

Whitman jammed his shoulder deeper into the pinned man's gut, shoving him hard onto the sword in his back. The tip of Clemf's blade burst from the man's chest, just above Whitman's head.

A second arrow, fired from ground level at point blank range, slipped through the eye slit in the man's helm to penetrate midshaft into his eye.

The soldier's sword slipped from his hand and hit the wet ground with a light splash. His limp body followed a moment after.

Regdar dropped his bow and grabbed the remaining soldier by the neckline of his breastplate. Lifting him to his feet, the big fighter shook the man.

"Tell me what you know about Naull."

The man cringed, trying to hold his broken shin. Beads of sweat dribbled down his forehead, and his eyes squeezed tightly shut.

Holding the man up with only one hand, Regdar knocked off his helm with the other.

"Talk to me, you slavemonger."

"Regdar—" started Whitman.

Regdar ignored the dwarf. Bending slightly at the knees, he lifted the captive into the air by his neck.

"I said talk!" He shook the man.

The soldier gurgled. He let go of his leg to claw at Regdar's hands.

"Regdar," shouted Whitman, "he couldn't talk now if he wanted to."

"Oh no?" shouted Regdar, still looking at the man he held more than a foot off the ground. He felt the dwarf's hand on his shoulder.

"You're killing him," insisted Whitman.

The soldier's clawing hands slowed, then dropped limply to his sides.

Regdar shook him one more time, then with a tremendous grunt, hurled the man into the air. The soldier flew backward and landed with a clatter a few feet from his fallen comrades. Regdar doubled over, breathing hard from the exertion. He looked at the tangled mess of a man lying still on the muddy ground.

Clemf bent down and put his fingers to the man's neck, then announced, "He's dead."

A cultist, wrapped from head to toe in black splintmail, pushed through the door to the blackguard's chamber.

"They've arrived at the edge of the swamp, my mistress," he announced.

The blackguard, hunched over a figure lying prone on a waist-high table, didn't bother to turn away from her work.

"That's good news," she said. "Keep me informed of their progress."

Tasca dropped softly down from the treetops, bow already stowed on his back.

Regdar straightened up. "Those men looked an awful lot like the ones who attacked the duke's keep."

Whitman scratched his beard, looking at the dead soldiers. "Maybe we should head back and inform the duke."

"No," shouted Regdar. He put his whole hand across his face, aware of how loud he had been. Then in a quieter voice, he said,

"You saw how they reacted when I mentioned Naull. She's here somewhere, and I'm going to find her."

Clemf stood up, finished with his inspection of the dead men. "Nothing," he declared, raising empty hands. "Not even a few coins."

"Professional soldiers," remarked Tasca. "Well-trained, well-outfitted, organized, and no nonsense. These aren't mercenaries. They have a purpose, a mission." He looked to Regdar, then to Whitman. "Even if we did return to alert the duke, then what? We'd just have to come back here, where the enemy is. Maybe we can kill two birds with one stone."

Regdar slapped the elf on the shoulder and nodded his agreement.

Clemf grabbed the first soldier by the arms and dragged him back toward the eel pool.

"If these soldiers are who we're looking for, and this is their swamp, then it's a good bet that we made enough noise killing these three to bring more of them." He looked up at his comrades.

Whitman and Regdar grabbed the other two and dragged them into the water as well. Tasca followed behind with a tree branch, sloshing mud back over their tracks and smoothing out the drag marks.

When the bodies were submerged, the group struck out again. The path they followed wound deeper into the swamp. Though it was mucky, it seemed to be the firmest patch of ground in the smelly wetland. Around two more bends, the dense vegetation gave way to a small clearing at the base of Mount Fear.

Seemingly built right out of the mountain, on the edge of that clearing, climbed an imposing black tower fortress. The walls rose from the base of the mountain up to the height of two storm giants. It jutted out of the mountain as if it were emerging from a deep slumber, stepping out into the swamp for the first time in hundreds of years.

Spires at the top leaned out, then angled back toward the mountain at the bottom so the fortress appeared unbalanced, as if it were surging forward, trying to break free of the restraining mountain.

A single door, wide enough to admit an ox cart, broke the smooth stone—the only opening on the ground level. Above that, Regdar counted twenty-four arrow slits cut into the wall, perhaps the height of two men from the ground. And at the very top, a wide balcony jutted out and overlooked the clearing before the fortress.

"Well, well, well," said Regdar. "What do we have here?"

"My money says somebody evil lives here," quipped Tasca.

"It certainly has an unwholesome look about it," agreed Whitman. "Look at all the spiky, jagged bits along the top edges."

"Black stone construction," added Clemf.

"Improbably placed in the middle of a dreary swamp with no safe access," confirmed Tasca.

"Yep," agreed Regdar. "It sounds like something out of a legend."

"Probably well guarded, too," cautioned Whitman.

"Maybe," replied Regdar, "but maybe not. Who do they expect to come prowling around, way out here? Anyone have a suggestion on how to proceed?"

Whitman hefted his hammer onto his shoulder and smiled. "I say let's do what we always do," replied the dwarf. "Kick down the door, kill whatever's inside, and haul away whatever's worth taking. Or in this case, rescue the girl. It's worked so far."

Tasca unsheathed his rapier. "That's the smartest thing you've ever said. We have a plan." He started toward the tower.

"Just one problem," interrupted Whitman.

Tasca stopped and turned around.

"They'll be able to smell you coming," said the dwarf. "Better let me lead."

"Planning on tunneling in?" quipped the elf.

"Only if I can use your pointy nose for a pick." Whitman pushed past and strode down the path.

"Oh, that was clever," replied Tasca. "Did you think that up all on your own, like the plan?"

"That's enough, you two," said Regdar. "Whatever we find in there is likely to be powerful enough to survive on the Elemental Plane of Fire. I can't be sure, but I'd say that's beyond anything I've ever killed." He turned to Whitman. "Do you honestly want to just march right up there, in the light of day, barge in, and hope they didn't see us coming?"

Whitman scratched his beard. "In a nutshell, yes."

Tasca quietly slipped his rapier into its sheath. "Only a dwarf would think up a numbskull idea like that."

Whitman smiled. "But only an elf would follow a numbskull." Then he turned to Regdar. "What do you propose we do?"

"We wait here until nightfall," said the fighter. "Then we go in, covered by darkness."

Clemf spoke up. "What about the guards we killed?"

"What about them?" asked Regdar.

"They're going to be overdue."

Regdar rubbed his chin, thinking. "Well," he said finally, lifting his fingers away from his face. "We kill two birds with one stone." He turned and headed back toward the pool. "We take their armor and sneak in, in disguise, assuming the eels left the bodies where we put them."

Whitman hefted his hammer over his shoulder. "I liked my idea better."

Regdar pulled one of the dead soldiers out of the water by his ankle.

"Nasty business, stealing a dead man's armor," he said, bending down to unfasten the first of many leather straps.

"Hey, look at this." Tasca had already removed most of one man's armor, exposing the dead soldier's upper body.

Regdar looked over the elf's shoulder as Whitman bent down and examined a large tattoo on the man's chest.

"These guys don't look like slavers," said the dwarf. "More like cultists."

"What makes you say that?" asked Regdar.

Whitman pointed to the tattoo.

"That's the mark of Hextor," he said, indicating the fist and arrows. "And those—" he pointed to three words inscribed above the image— "are words in Infernal."

"What do they say?"

The dwarf shook his head. "I don't know, can't read Infernal."

Tasca just shrugged.

"This one's got it too," said Clemf, having stripped down another of the dead soldiers.

Regdar returned to the man he'd pulled up. "Let's hope they're not checking tattoos at the door."

"Yeah," said Tasca. "Let's also hope we don't end up as sacrifices to the god of destruction."

"Cultists of Hextor don't sacrifice elves," said Whitman, putting on the first part of his stolen armor.

"Why not?" asked Tasca.

The dwarf smiled. "Waste of a good meal."

Newly outfitted in at least some pieces of black scale mail, Regdar and crew came hesitantly back to the edge of the clearing. Standing so near the tower nearly drove Regdar mad. Here he was, outside, while inside, he felt sure Naull was being tortured or worse. As far as he was concerned, they couldn't get inside fast enough.

"Do you think this is going to work?" asked Tasca.

Regdar shrugged. "Do you have a better idea?"

"Yeah," said Whitman. "We stop all this sneaking around and bust in."

"After you then." Regdar checked the hilt of his sword. "But no busting anything until I say the word. Remember, we want them to think we're on their side for now."

"Right," replied Whitman with a snort.

The dwarf marched toward the tower, and Clemf fell into step beside him. Regdar and Tasca followed close behind. The path they had been following led right up to the front gate. Heavy, wooden doors were held open by movable iron spikes along the entrance-way. The pointy, sharpened ends of a portcullis hung above. Below that, a heavy darkness descended, as if light itself were afraid to enter such a place.

"Here we go," whispered Tasca.

Regdar only nodded.

As they crossed the threshold, the man's eyes adjusted to the dim hallway. A handful of sconces holding dimly flickering torches lined the walls, which were made from the same black stone as the outside. The floor was covered in fine stone tiles alternating in dark and light shades, forming a checkerboard pattern.

The room they entered was long and wide, a grand foyer. It reminded Regdar of the duke's reception chamber or the entryway in the Church of Pelor back in New Koratia. It was the same, but different—designed for greeting newly arrived dignitaries but tainted with darkness. It seemed almost to mock itself, as if the whole room were simply a joke, a parody of good corrupted by evil.

There were no guards on duty, no reception party, and Whitman and Clemf continued on toward the wall at the far end of the long room. Regdar followed behind, focused on every detail, his senses aware of the light draft blowing in through the open door behind him and even the slight smell of swamp gas he'd all but grown accustomed to over the past few hours.

"I don't like this," he whispered. "Too easy."

Whitman nodded.

Tasca pulled out his bow.

A loud, skull-splitting, clanging sound echoed down the chamber. Regdar yanked his enchanted sword from its sheath and spun around.

Wrapped around a wooden wheel to the right of the chamber, a heavy chain was unwinding, and quickly. The portcullis thundered down to seal the entryway. Tasca took two quick steps toward the open door. Regdar flinched, knowing the elf would never make it through the gate in time.

As if the elf heard Regdar's thoughts, Tasca skidded to a stop. The portcullis hit the ground with a crash. Tiles cracked where the gate's sharp points slammed into them, and chips of stone were thrown in every direction.

"What have you done, elf?" shouted Whitman, his hammer already braced and ready for battle.

Tasca nocked an arrow to his bowstring, his eyes scanning every brick of the hall. "I followed your bumbling ass into a trap."

"Stop it," interrupted Regdar. "The disguises didn't work. Clemf, you're with me. Tasca and Whitman, stay together."

They nodded and paired off.

"And Whitman," said Regdar.

"Yeah?" replied the dwarf.

"Bust whatever you want."

"Right."

A grinding noise, sounding like stone on stone, echoed down the chamber. The wall at the far end parted. Regdar watched in amazement as the bricks slid back and disappeared into darkness. When the grinding stopped, the sound of heavy, marching boots filled the room.

Regdar looked to the other men. Whitman slapped his hammer against his hand with obvious impatience. Tasca sighted down his drawn arrow, watching the far wall. Clemf stood with his longsword held casually at his side, his eyes intently focused, his knees bent and ready to charge.

Regdar tested his grip on his greatsword and whispered a prayer under his breath. "Grant me the strength to vanquish my foes and carry my brethren through to safety," he said, stretching his neck to one side, then the other. "Woe be to those who oppose Pelor."

The darkness stirred, and from out of the newly formed portal in the wall poured a flood of black-clad soldiers.

Tasca let his arrow fly, and the first man to step into the flickering torchlight fell dead. Whipping his hand over his shoulder, he drew another arrow and fired again, dropping a second soldier.

The rushing enemy barely paused, however, and the room continued filling with black-armored warriors, like water gushing into a sinking boat. They marched uncaringly over their fallen comrades, flowing constantly forward.

"Whatever you do," shouted Regdar, "don't let them get behind us."

The others only had time to nod before the wall of black-armored soldiers came crashing down.

Whitman's hammer sent a clang echoing off the stone walls, disrupting the metered sound of the soldiers' marching. Tasca stood just behind the stalwart dwarf, firing arrows over his shoulder into the crowd of enemies.

Regdar and Clemf raised their swords over their shoulders and simultaneously cut into the line of men before them. The sound of metal against metal was followed by metal tearing flesh. Blood drenched the floor, and the swarm pushed forward.

Regdar ducked under a swing to his head then jammed the tip of his greatsword into his attacker's gut. The man grunted once, dropped his sword, and grabbed for his wound. Looking past the injured man, Regdar estimated the size of the small army he and his men faced. They were outnumbered easily four, maybe even five, to one.

Clemf slightly improved their odds when he connected with a two-handed swing. His blade plunged between the shoulder piece and helm of the man before him. The soldier's head slipped from his separated neck with a sickening pop. The headless body stood upright for a moment more, but Clemf never paused. His follow-through collided with another man's sword arm, slicing it off at the elbow.

The amputated body parts rolled on the floor, being trampled underfoot. Regdar saw a soldier step on the head. Its helm collapsed under the weight, and the skull made a loud cracking sound. The soldier lost his balance as the head caved in, and his other foot slipped on the gory flagstones.

Regdar's reverie was cut short by a slash to his leg. A pair of soldiers lunged at him from the side. There were so many he was having a hard time keeping track of them. One blade clanged harmlessly off his armor. The other cut into his muscle. The wound burned and made Regdar angry.

The big fighter rolled his hands over, bringing his enchanted blade to bear on the offending soldier. The weapon opened a large slice across the man's chest, cutting through metal, leather, and flesh alike.

The man hissed at the cut but stood his ground. His sword pulled back for another strike. Regdar stepped into the opening. He jabbed his elbow into the cut on the man's chest, scraping his jagged armor against the wound. The soldier shouted and fell to his knees, releasing his sword.

Regdar, smashed his knee into the man's face. The kneeling man reeled backward, swayed momentarily like a hypnotized snake, then collapsed.

Another man stepped in to take his place, rushing Regdar with his shoulder down. The soldier crashed into Regdar's chest and grabbed him in a bear hug. Regdar had leaped into the air when he saw the man coming, so the force of the impact carried both men backward several feet and out of the immediate fray. Regdar's weight was too much for the man to bear, however, and the attacker had to let him drop to the floor.

Regdar landed on his feet and took two long steps back to steady himself. His opponent was still off balance, so Regdar slammed his sword down with all his might against the top of the man's helmet. The blade struck with such force that it knocked him flat on his stomach. Regdar quickly stabbed the point through the gap below the man's helmet, cutting through his spine. Though the wound didn't kill him outright, the man lay on the floor unmoving, screaming at the top of his lungs.

Regdar was now separated from Clemf, and the tattooed human was surrounded. A black-clad soldier stepped behind him and jabbed a dagger at Clemf's unprotected flank. The dagger sank into Clemf's soft, fleshy backside, making him jump straight into the air.

Regdar charged back into the melee, zeroing in on the soldier stabbing at Clemf's rear. He took two steps before the sound of a bowstring filled his ears. He cringed, bracing himself for the impact.

The arrow wasn't aimed at Regdar. Green fletching sprouted in the ear of the man ahead. His knees went weak, and he spun around just in time to see Regdar before the greatsword knocked him to the floor with a blow to the chest. To his right, Tasca winked as he nocked another arrow and loosed it into the dwindling crowd.

Glad he's on my side, thought Regdar. He took a second to check on Whitman. The dwarf was flinging his hammer around in a figure eight pattern, bashing away blades and moving the soldiers back with his unorthodox style. Regdar had encountered men who had fought that way before. They had come from the far east, but they fought with small, finely crafted blades and trained for years in the ancient arts of swordplay. Somehow, seeing the dwarf use his hammer in the same fashion seemed comical—and effective.

Clemf stepped next to Regdar, rubbing his behind.

Another rumble echoed through the great hall—the sound of more marching soldiers.

The remaining fighters before Regdar and his men suddenly disengaged, falling back and forming a defensive line.

Tasca continued firing arrows into their midst, but now many of them were bashed away by blades or shields.

As they waited, the darkness at the far end of the room stretched and grew, widening along the edges, rolling out into the open and snuffing what light dared enter. Bits of that growing shadow broke off and separated into individual, man-sized chunks.

Regdar shook his head. It wasn't a shadow at all. It was an even bigger unit of black-clad soldiers.

"This doesn't look good," said Regdar.

"Not good at all," agreed Whitman.

The soldiers filled the room, forming ranks behind the defensive line. They stood for a moment, completely still. Only the sound of Tasca's arrows clanking off splint mail or sinking into flesh broke the silence.

As a group, the soldiers raised their swords.

Regdar stepped up beside Clemf. Tasca and Whitman did the same, forming a short line of their own.

The big fighter took a deep breath. He'd faced a lot of men in battle. Some were scared, some cool and confident. Then there were those who didn't care whether they lived to fight another day. It was those sorts who were the most dangerous.

Regdar looked at the eyes of the men standing before him— cultists of the god Hextor. They glared back, hard and cold. These men had no fear of death. They would come and come and come until they either won or all were dead. Regdar was sure of that.

They came.

Metal clanged on metal. Feet shuffled, and in the first few seconds, as soldiers clashed, men died.

Regdar and Clemf killed the first two, each with one swing.

Whitman slew two more on his own, and Tasca dropped one to his knees with an arrow to the gut. But for every one they removed from the line, another took his place. Rank upon rank moved forward. They filled the whole room, pushing away the light as a storm cloud blots out the sun. Regdar and his men were surrounded, fighting back to back.

Tasca dropped his bow and whipped out his rapier. He stood back to back with Whitman, slapping away blades with a zigzagging pattern. Whitman twirled his hammer, doing the same from the front.

Clemf spun around to protect Regdar's flank. Regdar smiled to himself at the thought of Clemf being stabbed twice in the ass in the same combat. There was no time for amusement, though. Swords flashed so quickly Redgar could barely track them. The attackers were so numerous that they interfered with each other. He and his companions, on the other hand, could attack almost anything that moved. Ferocity was their best protection, and they used it to its fullest advantage. They slashed and stabbed in all directions, heedless of the risks, trusting in raw aggression and each other to protect their backs.

As he bashed a blade into the air, stars burst across Regdar's field of vision, and he fell to one knee. A soldier stood over him with a mace raised for another shot at his head.

The mace swept down just as Regdar twisted his head away. It connected with the side of the helmet. The impact and the ringing clatter rattled the fighter. Pain shot through his skull, as if his brain were swelling and pressing on the back of his eyeballs, forcing them out of his head.

Focusing his eyes as best he could, Regdar tried to get back on his feet. The soldier hovering over him wound up for another blow. Regdar pulled back and tried to dodge. Silver flashed in front of his face, and the mace, still gripped by the man's gauntleted hand, dropped to the ground.

Behind the stunned, maimed cultist stood Clemf. Another quick stab with his sword killed the soldier whose fist he'd just amputated. Clemf then grabbed Regdar by the scruff of his neck and lifted him to his feet.

Desperate for anything that could buy them time, Regdar shouted at the top of his lungs, "Surrender! Surrender!"

The fighting ceased almost immediately. All of the attackers took a step back, but they didn't reform ranks. They just stood silently, surrounding Regdar and his men.

Regdar stood up tall, breathing hard, and adjusted his armor.

Whitman had a cut along his forehead. Clemf had dozens of small wounds across his arms and chest. None of them appeared serious, but he was covered in blood. Tasca, on the other hand, was completely untouched. It's good to be quick, Regdar thought.

Over the noise of shuffling soldiers and creaking armor came the sound of a set of heavy boots. The soldiers parted, creating a pathway from the far wall all the way to Regdar and his men. A single figure approached out of the darkness.

Tall, thick, and heavily armored, whoever it was obviously wore full plate mail. Black spikes jutted from the figure's shoulders, knees, and forearms. The mysterious person stepped out of the shadows into the light.

"We meet again," said a deep, gravelly voice.

Regdar narrowed his eyes. There before him, whole and unscathed, stood the blackguard whom he had battled in the City of Fire—the last person he'd seen standing beside Naull.

The big fighter snapped. Roaring his pain and fury, he charged at the blackguard, arms pumping, legs straining with every ounce of strength he had.

The soldiers moved to intercept him. Regdar cut them down. His blade carved a path through the wall of bodies before him. He was two steps beyond the slain before their bodies hit the floor.

Black-clad warriors converged on the enraged fighter, packing themselves against him so tightly that he couldn't move. His forward momentum came to a lurching stop, and Regdar could only push against the surging mass. The soldiers held their ground.

"It's nice to see you again, too," said the blackguard. She laughed. "It's almost flattering. He shows so much rage, yet he doesn't even know my name."

"No," replied Regdar, "but I know how long you have left to live."

The blackguard lifted her hands in the air to indicate the darkened chamber where they stood. "We're in the grand entrance hall." She smiled. "This is the perfect place for introductions." She bowed. "I am Lindroos, Blackguard of Hextor."

Regdar leaned back, then lunged forward. The press of bodies was so tight he couldn't swing his sword, but he could jab with it like a spear. He used the weapon to fell several more soldiers between himself and Lindroos before she halted him with her voice.

"Regdar," she said, "stop killing for a moment and hear me."

Regdar stepped back, glaring at the woman. "How do you know my name?"

The blackguard smiled. "There's someone I'd like you to meet." She spun sideways and lifted her arm in the air, revealing the dark passageway behind her.

Naull stepped quietly out of the gloom.

Regdar's knees went momentarily weak, but then his blood boiled. "Let her go," he bellowed.

Naull walked slowly across the tiles, stopping beside the blackguard. She placed her slender hand on Lindroos's shoulder, then wrapped her arms around the woman completely.

Lindroos put her hand on the back of Naull's head, leaned down, and pressed her lips to the wizard's in a passionate kiss. When they finished, the blackguard ran her finger across Naull's cheek. Both women smiled.

"To answer your question, Regdar—" Lindroos squeezed Naull closer to her with one arm— "I know your name because we have a mutual friend."

The two women smiled at each other, then turned and walked together back down the darkened corridor.

An arrow clanged from the pauldron of the blackguard's armor as she and Naull disappeared into the shadows, then they were gone.

Regdar's heart was gripped by a terrible, icy hand. His skin tingled, and a shiver ran up his spine. He rotated his wrists, feeling the finely wrapped hilt of his enchanted blade.

It felt good.

Dropping his shoulder, Regdar crashed headlong into the line of black-clad warriors. Three of them flew backward, tumbling others to the floor with them. Blades glanced off Regdar's armor, but he ignored them. Only moving forward mattered.

Tasca's arrows sailed overhead, striking sparks from metal armor and spurts of blood from exposed flesh. Regdar grabbed the shaft of an arrow that was stuck in a man's throat and yanked. The barbed arrowhead came out with a huge chunk of flesh attached. The man's eye's rolled back in his head, and he tried to staunch the rush of blood with his hands as he slid to the ground.

A cacophony rose through the room, rebounding from the black stones and doubling over on itself, gaining volume as it did. Metal clanged on metal. Boots trooped across stone, and the involuntary groans of men fighting and dying filled the air.

Clemf fought with both hands, cutting down soldiers with his blade and punching with his fist. Surrounded, he cut and slashed with the blinding speed of a hungry jungle cat, astoundingly fast for such a big man.

Whitman had tumbled backward, knocking the men flanking him to the ground. With a shout to activate his magical boots of speed, the stout dwarf got to his feet and finished the job, denting helms and pounding skulls into pulp. He'd been wounded severely across the face and chest. His breathing was labored and his fighting seemed to slow. Still, he fought on with ferocious might.

Tasca finally had to relinquish his bow when the soldiers pressed in too close. He switched to his rapier, dancing and weaving with what little space he had. Though he was quick, the limited room hindered him, and now he too was bleeding from many small cuts.

Bodies littered the floor. Regdar found himself balancing atop a dead man. Though the soldier's body provided little stability, the extra few inches of height were an advantage. Bashing aside one blade after another, Regdar leaped from the dead man and brought his sword down in a heavy chop. Two swords hit the floor in a tangle, their wielders' hands still gripping the hilts.

The soldiers stepped back, gripping the bleeding stumps where their wrists used to be. Regdar kicked out to his right and lunged forward with his greatsword to the left, like a dancer performing for the duke. Both men fell to the floor, where Regdar quickly finished them off.

At that moment, the room fell silent.

Breathing hard, Regdar looked up toward the far wall of the chamber. Not a single black-clad soldier remained in his way. He glanced back at the closed portcullis. Clemf was pulling his longsword from the body of a fallen soldier, Whitman was down on one knee, having a hard time breathing, and Tasca was seated on top of a bleeding but still-living soldier.

"Where have they gone?" quizzed the elf. He held the tip of a dagger at the soldier's throat.

The man shook his head.

"I said," repeated the elf, pushing his blade deeper into the warrior's skin, "where have they gone?"

The man reached up, obviously in pain, and grabbed Tasca's wrist. The elf realized the man's intent too late. Before he could wrest the dragger away, the soldier plunged it into his own neck up to its hilt. Blood frothed out of the wound and the man's mouth, then the soldier's head slumped to the side.

Whitman had watched the suicide with calm exhaustion. "It's all your fault, elf," he said, almost coughing on the words. "If you'd been a better shot, she wouldn't have gotten away."

Tasca stowed his rapier, uncorked a silvery flask, and handed it to Whitman.

"If you hadn't been so ugly, she probably wouldn't have wanted to leave so quickly."

The dwarf downed the potion in one long gulp. The wound on his forehead immediately stopped bleeding, and the blood dried into a scaly scab. He dropped the empty flask and slapped Tasca on the arm.

"Who says I wanted her around anyway." The dwarf smiled. Hefting his hammer over his shoulder, he stepped over a dead soldier and headed for the other side of the room.

He looked back over his shoulder. Regdar and Clemf were downing potions of their own.

"Well," said Whitman in a rather gruff voice, "are you two going to stand there and drink all day, or are we going after the bitch?"

Clemf tossed away his empty flask. "That's not a very nice thing to say about Regdar's woman."

Whitman stopped altogether and turned around. He leaned forward, toward the tattooed human, and narrowed his eyes.

"Not Regdar's woman, you oaf. The blackguard." He shook his head and continued climbing over the dead. "If you weren't so enormous, I'd have no use for you." He flung his head back. "You know that?"

Tasca grabbed Clemf's arm as he passed. "Welcome to my own personal plane of Hell," he said.

Regdar, Clemf, and Tasca followed the dwarf to the shadowy end of the room. There they discovered that the black bricks and the darkness had concealed from them a narrow passageway that led deeper into the fortress. Whitman proceeded into the pitch-black hallway, but slowly as if looking for something.

"Hold up there, you sewer rat," chided Tasca. "The humans can't see in the dark."

"You can't see in the dark," replied the dwarf, and he continued searching in the darkness.

Tasca turned toward Regdar and Clemf. "Hold on," he said, nodding.

The elf walked a short distance back into the room, along the wall. Above him, suspended about twice his height in a black iron sconce, hung one of the lit torches that lined much of the chamber. Squatting down on his haunches, he leaped into the air. Easily passing the torch on his way up, Tasca shoved on its shaft to knock it free. Pushing off the wall at the height of his jump, the elf grabbed the tumbling torch on his way down before landing softly on both feet.

He handed it to Clemf with a bow.

The tattooed human accepted the torch. "How do you do that?"

Tasca winked. "I'm part frog."

Regdar grabbed the elf's right hand and lifted it up. "He has a ring of jumping," indicating the plain-looking band on Tasca's finger. He let go of the elf's hand and grabbed the torch from Clemf. "Come on."

Regdar headed into the dark corridor, following after Whitman.

The hallway continued in a straight line deeper into the mountain. The passage was much smaller than the grand entrance hall, and any resemblance this building had to other, more regal palaces stopped at the end of that enormous chamber. Water seeped through cracks between bricks to run in rivulets across the floor. Where the water collected in small puddles, slippery algae grew in patches matching the shape of the puddle above it. The damp corridor gave off a musty, stagnant smell.

Ahead of Regdar, Whitman crouched, his hammer on the floor beside him. He was examining the base of the wall.

Regdar came up behind the squatting dwarf. "Find something?"

"Yep." Whitman's hand disappeared into a depression in the brick. The wall slid away, grinding against the stone floor as it did. As the wall opened, light creeped around the brick, flickering weakly into the hallway.

Whitman stood up and retrieved his hammer.

Clemf and Tasca stepped up behind Regdar, their weapons at the ready. Whitman looked at each of them in turn, nodded, then headed into the room.

The chamber Whitman had revealed was small, maybe large enough for twenty to twenty-five armed and armored men to stand side by side without bumping into each other. The ceiling was perhaps the height of two dwarves, one standing on the other's shoulders.

On the far wall, two lit torches flickered in heavy, iron sconces. The flickering light played through masses of cobwebs along the walls, revealing the bony remains of perhaps a dozen long-dead soldiers on the floor. Dust and bits of cobweb covered the exposed bones and rusted armor.

Whitman took a step inside the room, kicking up a plume of dust as he did. The dwarf sneezed. The booming noise echoed around the small room, bouncing from the stone walls and rolling down the long hallway.

Tasca whipped his bow around, pointing down the dark passage. He cocked his head, listening.

Whitman lifted his arm and wiped his face with his sleeve.

He looked back at Regdar. "Sorry. Dust."

The big fighter nodded. "Your sneezes could wake the dead."

As if on cue, the chamber began moving. Rusted armor clanked and scratched as the bones of dead, human fighters lifted themselves off the floor and prepared to fight.

Regdar stepped into the room to stand next to Whitman. He heard a twang, and an arrow whipped over his shoulder. The projectile passed directly through a skeleton's ribcage, flying harmlessly between the exposed bones and shattering against the stone wall behind.

The animated bones shambled forward. Whitman swung his hammer with a pounding blow. His target's skull, encased in a rusted helm, collapsed like brittle parchment. The hammer traveled on, unslowed, crushing ribs, spine, hip, and femur. Spiked bits of shattered bone flew all over the room as the creature exploded from the force of Whitman's attack.

Regdar swept his greatsword overhead in a one-handed strike. The sharp blade clove through a skeleton's shoulder with a sharp, cracking sound. The monster shambled on, minus its right arm.

A mass of rusted blades and sharp finger bones jabbed at Regdar and Whitman. Harsh scraping noises filled the chamber as the attacks scratched down the fighters' armor. The rattling of bones and the shuffling of feet continued as the undead pressed on.

Regdar stepped farther into the room, simply shoving three skeletons back with his extended arm. Clemf stepped in behind him, taking the spot directly beside Whitman. His longsword cut right through one skeleton at the waist and knocked the head from another. The thing continued lurching forward, unfazed by the lack of a skull.

Tasca let fly with another round of arrows, more carefully aimed than before. His first lodged in the spine of a skeleton in the back rank. The creature seemed unaffected at first but then its knees wobbled, and it fell, once again lifeless, to the floor. The second arrow struck dead center on a monster's pelvis. The shaft vibrated as the skeleton shambled on, the arrow pointing stiffly where the creature was headed.

Whitman's hammer never paused. The head struck one skeleton and knocked it into a second, sending both to the floor in a broken pile. Shifting one step to his left, the dwarf swung again, and a spine-tingling crunch scattered more bones across the floor.

The skeletons fought on, mindlessly scratching and hacking as best they could, but not a single blow landed on Regdar or his crew. Their heavy armor and fighting prowess kept them safe. In less than a minute, the long-dead soldiers were once again at rest, this time safely in bits and pieces.

Besides the rusted weapons, cobwebs, and broken skeletons, the room yielded nothing of worth, and the men continued down the passageway.

Several paces farther, on the same side of the hall, Whitman found a rotten wooden door, banded together with long, black lengths of iron. The hanging ring that served as a handle had long-since fallen off, and the hinges were rusted.

Holding an arrow nocked and ready, Tasca stood against the opposite wall. Regdar held the torch and his greatsword, his back against the wall beside the door. With those two in position, Whitman and Clemf grabbed hold of the old door and heaved.

The door came apart in their hands. Splinters of rotten wood and bits of rusted metal collapsed to the floor with hardly a crack or creak. On the other side, the chamber Whitman and Clemf had revealed was completely dark. The stench of rotten flesh and rancid blood wafted into the hall. All four of the men cringed back from the smell, covering their noses with their sleeves.

Whitman and Clemf readied themselves, and Regdar turned the corner, holding his breath as he entered the room.

The light from the fighter's torch illuminated a room about twice the size of the last one. Along the walls stood the dilapidated remains of a once-functional torture chamber. Iron maidens, racks, shackles, and other implements of despair littered the chamber. As Regdar crossed father into the room, he saw the dried-up outlines of brown pools of blood. Most of the floor was stained to some extent. The color of stone on the worked-tile floor was the exception, not the rule.

In the middle of the chamber stood an unusual device. To Regdar, it looked like a heavy, wooden chair attached to a smallish catapult. The chair had metal straps on the arms, legs, and back. Whoever or whatever was unfortunate enough to be put in this throne of woe wasn't meant to get out.

The back of the chair was attached to a pair of thick wooden beams that extended above the seat. At the top of these beams, a heavy metal and wood structure was bolted between them. It looked as if it could move back and forth, balanced between the two beams. Had it been closer to the ground, it could have been a child's seesaw.

Above the chair, bolted to the suspended seesaw, was another metal strap—the same construction as the ones meant to hold a person's arms and legs into the chair. The opposite side of the balanced structure held a leather basket—woven in the shape of a spider's web—full of large stones. That end rested on the ground.

The four men spread out, looking at this odd device.

"What in the nine planes of Hell is that?" blurted Whitman.

Clemf shook his head.

"Beats me," replied Regdar.

Tasca stepped up to it, tilting his head to the side. "That, my good and excellent friends, is something I hoped I would never see in my lifetime." The elf circled around the huge machine. "My father used to tell me tales of a tribe of dark elves, drow, who would capture young wood elves who didn't obey their parents. Each time he told the story, he changed it a little bit. Sometimes the dark elves would eat the bad little children, other times they would simply enslave them." Tasca finished his circle around the grisly creation. "Once, when I was getting a little older, and I'd gotten into more serious trouble, he told me that the drow would come that night and take me away. He claimed they would torture me, and he even went so far as to explain this very machine to me."

The other three men stood silently, listening.

"It's called the Spider's Bite." He turned and walked to the chair. "The intended victim is strapped in, and the boom is lowered so the restraint can be put around his neck." The elf stepped up onto the seat of the chair. Reaching up, he tugged on the metal collar bolted to the end of the boom. "Once it's secure, the torturer puts rocks in the basket." He stepped down and began walking out of the room. "There is a point," he continued, "when the disks in the spine begin separating and the bones pull away from the ribs they attach to. Much past that point, and a man's head will be torn right off his shoulders, sometimes with the spine still attached."

The other three followed him out of the torture chamber.

"Your father told you about this machine—as a child?" asked Regdar.

Tasca continued down the hall, simply nodding his head.

"Your father was a bastard," said the big fighter.

Tasca continued nodding.

The band of fighters made their way down the rest of the passage. At the end they found a final door, much like the last they'd entered, but this one was in much better shape. Though the wood was old and the metal tarnished, the hinges weren't rusted, and the dirt on the floor had been disturbed recently.

"This must be the place," said Regdar.

The others agreed, and they took up the same positions as last time. On Regdar's nod, Clemf and Whitman peeled open the door. A warm glow filled the passageway and a light wind blew dust into the air.

Regdar stood with his back against the wall, the torch flickering in his hand. He looked out at Tasca, his bow trained on the opening. The elf's eyes shifted back and forth, searching, then they settled on something inside the chamber, and they grew to twice their size.

That was all the big fighter needed to see.

Tasca let his arrow fly, and Regdar spun around the corner, following the projectile.

One step inside the door, he stopped and looked up. The torso, arms, and head of a huge, muscular man floated in the air before him. Where the man's legs should have been, a mass of dust and air whipped around in a swirling storm. The creature glared down at Regdar, its beady eyes set deep within its bald skull. It crossed its arms, setting its elbow on the hilt of a tremendous falchion. Tasca's arrow rested on the floor.

"You must be Regdar," said the floating half-man in a booming voice.

A heavy wind blew through the room, and Regdar's torch flickered feebly. He dropped it and gripped the hilt of his sword in both hands.

"And you must be an efreeti," replied the big fighter.

The swirling creature nodded, the long hairs of its beard whipping about its head.

Clemf and Whitman took up positions on either side of Regdar.

"I don't suppose you're going to grant us three wishes," said Regdar.

"No," replied the efreeti with a smile, "but I admire your spirit."

The efreeti raised its hand, its fingers almost touching the ceiling. A huge ball of flame erupted in its palm, further illuminating the room that was already brightly lit simply by the fiery creature's presence.

Tasca sighted down his bow, taking aim at the outsider.

"This is bad," said Regdar.

Tasca released his arrow. The projectile struck the efreeti in the shoulder, and the large outsider roared. Its brow furrowed, and the flame flickered in its hand.

Tasca reached for another arrow.

You'll pay for that, elf. The efreeti's voice boomed through Tasca's head.

The flame in the floating creature's hand raged again, never having fully gone out, and the efreeti hurled the glowing glob at Tasca.

Regdar, Whitman, and Clemf all ducked as the flaming orb surged over their heads. The magical fire impacted the sturdy wooden door, splashing into a puddle of flame and dripping down onto the floor.

Clemf ended up in a heap on the ground, his hair singed. The big, tattooed human clattered around on the stone as he tried to regain his feet.

Regdar was the first to recover his wits, and he charged in, his greatsword held high. Slicing the blade down in a smooth, natural arc, Regdar leaned into the charging strike. His enchanted weapon glowed brightly as it struck the efreeti's hide. Arcane marks of power glittered as the blade bit deep into fiery flesh.

Whitman tumbled into the fray, dodging behind the large creature and taking up a position opposite Regdar. He wheeled with his hammer, crashing the head of his weapon into the outsider's flank. The dwarven metal sparked as it connected, growing red-hot against the fiery creature's flesh.

The efreeti grumbled, and its lip curled in a sneer. Tasca trained an arrow on its chest, adjusted for the magical wind, and let fly. The projectile impacted the outsider squarely in the shoulder, but the efreeti didn't even flinch. Instead it spun to face the dwarf behind it. As it turned, Tasca could see the shaft of his arrow burst into flames.

The magical fire in the efreeti's palm suddenly went out, and the creature began uttering something in a language Tasca didn't recognize. With a final, booming syllable, the towering monster clapped its hands together, and the floor before it erupted in flame. The fire filled one side of the room from wall to wall, floor to ceiling.

A sudden jolt ran up Tasca's spine. "Whitman!"

The wall of flame had appeared directly on top of where the stubborn dwarf had been standing.

The efreeti spun back around, a smug look on its face.

Clemf managed to get back to his feet and charge. His blade connected with the creature's wrist and skipped along its arm, finally sinking into the upper part of the efreeti's shoulder. An oozing, pitchlike substance seeped out of the wound. When Clemf withdrew his weapon, the goo ignited, sticking to his blade. The tattooed human stood before the efreeti, flaming sword in hand, breathing hard from the heavy strike.

Regdar, with his back turned to Tasca, lifted his greatsword for an overhead hack. The efreeti pulled a falchion from the swirling clouds below its waist and with a quick stroke, deflected Regdar's blow. Regdar shifted, and stepped forward in an unbalanced lunge. His sword struck the hilt of the outsider's blade, but its momentum slid the weapon up and in, jamming the sharp point into the monster's gut.

The creature let out a terrific roar and pulled its hand to its stomach. The swirling maelstrom that supported the monster's naked chest, arms, and head stopped spinning. The breeze in the room came to an end, and the efreeti's legs appeared. Looking down at the wound Regdar had inflicted, the outsider laughed. It removed its hand from the inconsequential scratch and gripped its falchion with both hands.

A tremendous, warbling cry arose from the fiery magic wall. It echoed off the worked stone and overtopped every sound in the room. The unnerving shout was followed by a twirling ball that shot straight out of the fire. The ball twisted and tumbled, arcing through the air.

Out of the tangle emerged a flaming, very pissed-off dwarf.

Whitman's beard was singed, and the ends were still alight. His lip curled up in a terrible sneer, and his eyes blazed with hatred. The sight sent a chill down Tasca's spine.

"You overgrown mephit," roared Whitman. "Your days of roasting dwarves are over."

Shouting out the power word for his boots, Whitman accelerated. Hammer and dwarf gained momentum as they charged the efreeti, then the head of the magical silver hammer impacted its target. A skull-rattling boom shook dust from the ceiling. It was as if Whitman were a bolt of lightning instead of an angry, mortal dwarf.

The efreeti stumbled back, obviously shaken by the blow, and the fiery wall behind it dropped away into nothingness. The room became much darker, lit only by the glowing outline of the outsider.

Tasca trained another arrow on the monster and let fly. His well-placed shot struck the efreeti in the forehead. The beast recoiled another step.

Clemf and Regdar seized the opportunity to rain stabs and slashes against the creature. More flaming pitch oozed from wounds on the efreeti's tremendous body.

The magical being shook its head as if to clear it, stepped forward, and sliced its falchion down in a flailing, two-handed strike. The weapon struck Regdar in the chest, knocking him backward.

Regdar's arms flew outward, and his legs left the ground. With a riotous clang, he landed on his seat and skidded across the floor. He remained upright for a moment more, then he crashed to his back, spread-eagle on the floor.

Regdar had watched the efreeti's falchion hit him squarely in the chest. He felt himself lifted from the ground. Now he was on his back and not sure how he'd gotten there. His chest hurt, but that was nothing new. His chest had hurt since the day he'd lost Naull in the City of Fire.

That pain had dulled a little over time, but seeing her again brought it back, stronger than he remembered it ever being. It burned with new fury as he watched Lindroos kiss and caress her. Under other circumstances, he might have enjoyed that kiss, but now, it hurt like hell.

He looked down at himself. There's blood on my armor, he thought. He looked up. The room wavered and swirled. Was that another of the efreeti's tricks? The efreeti was gone from his vision, and he could no longer focus on anything. He heard the back of his helmet hit the floor before blacking out.

Hollering with what must have been all the air in his lungs, Whitman hurled his hammer at the efreeti. The toss lifted the little man off his feet. In the dwarf's ears, the room was silent except for the whooshing sound of the hammer rotating end over end as it flew toward the monster. That sound was followed by a heart-dropping clap and grind as the hilt struck the floor, and the weapon skidded harmlessly away from its target.

The efreeti laughed and stepped toward Whitman, leering down from nearly twice the dwarf's height.

"I'll roast who I choose, little morsel," it thundered.

Tasca pulled a single, blue-tipped arrow from his quiver and nocked it to his bow. "Not today."

Sighting down the bow, the elf whispered a single word. Magical light flashed out over the arrow, forming tiny, blue crystals along its shaft, tipped in a frosty white. He released the string.

The arrow jumped across the room like a thunderbolt. The head of the projectile impacted against the efreeti's chest, and an explosion of light surrounded the monster. Bits of ice and flakes of snow swirled in a magical pool of mixed purples and blues, and the room went suddenly cold.

Fingers of crystallized ice reached out and wrapped themselves around the efreeti, squeezing it like a giant hand. The fingers grew as they cascaded over the monster's shoulders and chest. The efreeti squirmed, and dropped its blade. As the icy cold enveloped its head, it let out a terrific howl that echoed and re-echoed until the room vibrated with the intensity of it.

Tasca lowered his bow. The efreeti was entirely encased in a glistening sarcophagus of blue-white ice. Its features were frozen and distorted—the face was still fearsome, but the eyes were frozen in a terrified stare.

The room was now almost completely dark, lit only by the barely flickering flame of Regdar's discarded torch. The three men looked at the frozen giant for a moment more before Whitman—the flames in his beard now extinguished—bolted over to Regdar, lying prone on the floor. Tasca crossed over as well, while still keeping one wary eye on the efreeti.

Regdar lay motionless on his back with a large wound across his chest. Even though his arms were flung straight out to his sides, he had managed to keep a grip on his greatsword.

Whitman knelt beside him.

Clemf rubbed his hand over his face. "Is he alive?"

Whitman put his hand to Regdar's throat. The dwarf cocked his head to the side, almost as if he were listening for something.

"Well?" asked Tasca.

Whitman remained quiet for a long moment.

Tasca kicked the dwarf in the back. "Hey, you little oaf, I asked you a question. Did that fire burn out your tongue along with your beard?"

"No," replied Whitman.

Clemf's sword clattered to the ground.

For the second time since they had opened the door to this room, Tasca felt his heart miss a beat. He lowered his head.

"No," repeated Whitman, "he's not 'well'. Give me a potion."

A thrill ran down Tasca's spine. Dropping everything, the elf flung his pack from his back and dug frantically inside for a healing potion. Flasks clanked together as he fished around. Pulling out a vial, the elf shoved it at the dwarf.

Whitman uncorked the bottle, cradled up Regdar's head from the floor, and poured the magical liquid down his throat. Half way through the bottle, the human fighter coughed and gagged. His arms came to life, flailing around like a drowning sailor's. Whitman pulled back, keeping the rest of the potion in the bottle, as Regdar gasped for air.

Clemf picked up his sword, then walked over next to Whitman. He leaned down, putting his face right next to the dwarf's.

"I don't claim to understand the little games you and the elf play," he said. "Sometimes the two of you even amuse me with your constant bickering." He leaned in even closer, his nose touching Whitman's. "But if you ever again joke like that about someone dying, I'll cut your beard off—and maybe I'll leave it attached to your face."

Whitman swallowed hard but remained silent.

Tasca held his breath, not quite sure what to make of the exchange.

"So we understand each other?" asked Clemf.

Whitman raised his eyebrows and nodded.

"Good." Clemf leaned back, slapped the dwarf on the shoulder, and broke out laughing.

Tasca sighed and chuckled. "For a quiet guy, you're pretty funny."

Clemf smiled. "You think so?"

"Yeah," interjected Whitman, "a real riot."

Regdar woke up coughing.

Whitman stood over him with an uncorked vial in his hand. Clemf stood over the dwarf, saying something into his face.

Regdar gagged and gulped for air. The other three were laughing.

"Oh," said Regdar between gasps, "so when I die, it's funny?"

Whitman shook his head and handed Regdar the half-full flask. "I'm going to poke around." The dwarf left the room, headed back down the corridor.

Regdar downed the rest of the healing potion, then fished in his pack for another one.

Tasca picked up the torch and scanned the walls. "It's possible they teleported out of here so that we'd just come to a dead end. This is the last openly accessible room on this level."

Clemf agreed. "Even if we do find a hidden stairway or a secret door, this whole thing is probably some elaborate trap." He walked up and helped Regdar get back to his feet. "Besides, pardon me for being honest, but your woman didn't exactly seem thrilled to see you."

Regdar gritted his teeth and glared at Clemf. "That wasn't Naull." His expression softened. "It looked like Naull, but it must have been an illusion or a doppelganger or . . . or I don't know what, but it wasn't Naull."

"Okay. All right." Clemf held up his hands in front of him, showing his palms to Regdar in a sign of nonaggression. "Just calm down and think about this for a minute. If it wasn't Naull, then what are we doing here?"

"If you hadn't noticed," replied Regdar, feeling rather indignant, "the black-armored men we fought in the entry hall were outfitted and uniformed exactly like the ones who attacked the duke's keep."

"Really?" said Clemf. "I thought black was just a fashionable color for evil minions, whatever the season." The tattooed man shook his head. "Didn't we cover this before?"

Regdar ignored the jibe. "It's likely that blackguard, Lindroos, is the person behind the attack at the keep. She's certainly in charge of the soldiers here, and if they're all on the same side, then by staying here and defeating them we're defending New Koratia." He straightened himself up. "Besides, Naull or not, that blackguard is the last person I saw alive with her, so she knows what happened." He looked Clemf right in the eye. "I intend to find out the truth."

Tasca finished searching and returned to the other two. "Personally, Regdar, you know I'm always up for a fight." He shrugged. "But in this case, I've got to side with Clemf. If the blackguard is behind the attack on the duke's keep, and if there's more to her plan, then we should go back and alert the duke." He looked Regdar in the eye. "We can come back with the rest of the army."

Regdar put his hands to his temples, massaging the wrinkles in his forehead. "We can't go back," he said.

Clemf laughed. "Of course we can go back. It's just a few days walk. . . ."

Regdar shook his head.

Tasca narrowed his eyes. "What do you mean, 'we can't go back'?"

Regdar threw his hands in the air. "We can't go back, okay!" he shouted. He turned around and began pacing. "The duke, he . . ."

"The duke what?" Clemf took a step forward, his fists clenched.

Regdar looked at him and shrugged. "The duke . . . the duke told me I couldn't leave. He never gave his permission. In fact, he said that if I came out here looking for Naull, then I could never return to New Koratia." His eyes shifted from Clemf to Tasca and back again. "I resigned my commission."

Clemf took another step forward. "You told us we had the duke's blessing." He grabbed Regdar by the collar. "We came out here with you as a favor, risked our lives for you, and you lied to us!" The tattooed human shook the big fighter, nearly lifting him off his feet. Clemf's face turned red, and spittle flew from the corners of his lips. "The duke thinks we abandoned our posts, Regdar." He shook the big fighter again, spraying saliva in his face as he talked. "Our careers as soldiers are over." Regdar's armor clattered louder as Clemf became more violent. "We left our homes, and now we can't even go back—and for what? To chase a dead woman!" Clemf's lips curled up in a sneer, and he thrust Regdar backward, pushing him hard to the ground. "You lying—" Clemf fished around for the right words. "We trusted you with our lives." He took a menacing step forward.

Tasca stepped up and put his hand on the man's tattooed arm, but Clemf pulled away, continuing to menace the fallen fighter.

Regdar just looked up from the ground, not bothering to even try to get up.

"You're right," said Regdar. "You're right."

Clemf pulled his fist back, winding up to punch Regdar in the face.

"As much as I'd like to do that myself," said Whitman, now leaning in the doorway, "there's not much we can do about it now. The only way we'll ever get back into New Koratia and clear our good names with the duke is if we stop this blackguard before she completes whatever wicked scheme she's concocted." He pushed off the door, hefting his hammer onto his shoulder. "If we bring Duke Ramas her head on a pike, he'll let us back in." The dwarf turned and headed back down the passage. "Come on," he said over his shoulder. "I found a stairway."

Regdar got up from the ground and dusted himself off. He headed out the door, avoiding Clemf's stare.

Whitman led the group to a spot on the unbroken northern wall of the passageway. He stopped, looked back at the other three men, then put his hand on the stone.

It passed right through.

"Illusion," said Regdar.

Whitman's hand, disguised by the illusionary wall up to the wrist, came back into view, and he waved Regdar forward.

The big fighter nodded and stepped into the imaginary stone. He felt his hand slip effortlessly through, then speckled black brick filled his vision, and for a split second, everything went dark. When his eyes emerged from the illusion, he had to squint to protect them from the bright light.

On the other side, a worked-stone arch marked the opening to a hallway. Torches lined the walls every few steps. Though it was bright, the illusion had blocked the light from illuminating the outer hallway. A stairway led up at the end of the hidden passage, rising so steeply that from where he stood, Regdar couldn't see the top.

The others came through the illusionary wall, and as a group the four men headed up the stairs with Regdar in the lead. Moving carefully onto the first step, the big fighter rose. Above him, the stairs climbed higher, the angle of the ceiling still preventing him from seeing where the stairway ended.

"I don't like this," he whispered, and he drew his sword.

The others followed suit.

For several tense moments, Regdar climbed, craning his neck as he did, trying as best he could to get a glimpse of what was up ahead. Silence enveloped the stairwell, broken only by the sounds of the flickering torches and the scuffling of four large men ascending the rough stone stairs.

Finally Regdar caught sight of the top. Five steps away, he could see darkness spread out over the last step. What lay beyond, he hadn't a clue. He stopped and turned back toward the others.

"I can see the top," he whispered into Whitman's ear. "Good place for an ambush."

Whitman nodded.

"We go up fast. They know we're here. No sense in trying to surprise them. Let's just minimize the danger to us." Regdar looked Whitman in the eyes then pointed to Tasca, standing one step below the dwarf.

Whitman nodded again and turned to the elf, repeating the message in his ear.

Tasca responded in kind, relaying the information to Clemf behind him.

When all three nodded to Regdar, he turned back toward the top step, took a deep breath, gripped his sword tightly in one hand, and charged.

His armor made a tremendous clank as he ascended two steps at a time. As his head breached the level of the landing, his right foot struck the second to last step with a loud click. Looking down the well-lit corridor, Regdar saw nothing but more hallway.

A moment later, stairs beneath the fighters' feet collapsed, turning into a steep, smooth chute, and Regdar tumbled backward.

Whitman cartwheeled to his right, kicking away from the falling fighter and spinning gracefully through the air. He reached out and caught hold of one of the sconces. Regdar fell underneath the acrobatic dwarf, clanging and crashing as he slid back toward the elf.

Tasca bent his knees and jumped forward, diving over the tumbling fighter toward the top of the chute. His midsection cleared Regdar, but his feet smacked into the back of the falling man's head. Landing on his stomach on the smooth chute, Tasca reached for the top lip where the end of the last stair used to be. His fingertips grazed the landing, but he slid backward with the tilt of the steep slope.

Regdar felt Tasca's feet hit the back of his head, and his arms flailed wide, reaching for anything that might stop his descent. He caught nothing, and he fell backward.

Clemf continued running forward, his feet slipping with every step. His body was in motion, but he made no progress, managing only to stay in place.

Regdar landed on his shoulders and struck his head against the ramp. His feet tumbled up and back over his twisted body. He somersaulted out of control backward down the chute. He saw the black stone ceiling, then his feet, then Clemf's comical, stationary run. When Regdar's feet collided with the tattooed human's chest, the two tangled up in a heap.

Limbs flailed. Armor crashed and clanked. All of the air in Regdar's lungs rushed out in a groaning whisper each time his back smacked against the floor. Clemf cursed in several languages.

At the bottom of the chute, both men tumbled out of the secret chamber, shooting through the illusion and smashing into the opposite wall. Regdar lay on the ground with his back bent against the stone. Clemf rested on his belly, unmoving.

A moment later the illusionary wall wavered, and Tasca flew out. He too landed facedown. He whimpered softly, then let himself collapse completely to the floor.

Regdar took stock of his body. His hands and forearms were scraped up pretty badly, and his head hurt. He felt around and discovered a number of bruises, but nothing seemed broken, and his injuries were minor. Lifting himself up on his haunches, he got to his feet.

By then, Clemf and Tasca were beginning to move. Both men moaned as they struggled to get up.

"Nice work, Regdar," spat Clemf as he checked himself out.

"And you would have known to avoid that step?" quipped Tasca. "We're lucky it was just a trap and not an ambush."

"Listen, Clemf," Regdar held his hands out, pleading, "I—"

"Save it," snapped the tattooed man, biting off his words as he stuck his upraised index finger in Regdar's face. "There's nothing you can say that's going to make me forgive you, so just keep out of my way, and for Pelor's sake, don't talk at me." Clemf spun around and limped back through the illusion.

"That went well," said Tasca.

Regdar wrinkled his forehead. "How come you're not mad at me?"

"I am," said the elf. "Eventually you'll have to sleep." Tasca smiled then turned and followed Clemf out of the hallway.

"Great." Regdar shook his head. He took a few moments to finish his personal examination before joining the others at the base of what used to be the stairway.

When he crossed through the illusion, Clemf was kneeling down and scratching at the stones on the floor. Tasca stood over him, looking up the chute.

"Whitman," Tasca whispered the dwarf's name. Receiving no answer, he repeated it a bit louder. He turned around and shrugged. "I don't think it's such a good idea to start yelling, but the last I saw, Whitman was hanging on to a torch sconce."

Regdar nodded toward the chute. "Do you think you could climb it?"

The elf nodded. "Yes, but not fast." Tasca looked down at Clemf. "Any luck?"

The tattooed fighter shook his head. "Just rocks. No lever." He stood up.

"Mechanism's probably at the top." Tasca scratched his chin. "Where the hell is Whitman."

A slapping sound echoed down the chute. All three men readied their weapons in a blink, and they stood, anxiously watching for whatever was coming down at them.

The noise grew louder, and Regdar squeezed the hilt of his sword. A shadow tumbled into view, skewed by the flickering torches. Regdar could hear the other men suck in their breath, then a long, brown, serpentine object unraveled at their feet.

Clemf lunged forward, smashing the thing with his sharp blade. His attack hit its mark, slicing right through. Sparks flew off the stone. A piece of the creature before them came off.

It wasn't a creature.

Tasca lowered his rapier. "It's a rope."

Clemf's cheeks flushed, and he sheathed his longsword. He opened his mouth to say something, but thought better of it and closed it again.

"Hurry up, will you," came Whitman's voice from down the chute. "We don't have all year."

Tasca sheathed his blade and grabbed the rope. He climbed up hand over fist, jamming the toe of his boot into the corner where the wall met the floor. In a few steps, he disappeared from view.

Regdar held his hand out and bowed his head. "After you."

Clemf glared up the twisting passage for a moment before grabbing hold of the rope and pulling himself up.

Regdar followed a few moments later, and shortly the entire group was reunited at the top. Whitman wound up his rope, shoved it in his pack, and slapped Regdar on the arm.

"This time, I'll lead." He smiled.

The dwarf led the party down another narrow, well-lit hallway. They took their time, examining the floor and the walls meticulously as they went. Though they were careful, they found nothing except a door at the end of the passage.

Unlike the dark hallway they explored below, this one didn't afford them the luxury of spreading out and taking cover while they opened the door.

"How does this go again?" asked Whitman, hefting his hammer to his shoulder. "Kick down the door, take the treasure, and kill the monster?"

"You got the door part right," said Tasca, nocking an arrow to his bowstring, "but you have to kill the monster first, then you take its treasure."

The dwarf smiled. "Maybe that's how *you* do it." Then he turned and kicked the door with all of his substantial might.

The wood and iron slammed away from the group, hinges protesting as it swung. Inside, a large, lighted room greeted them. At the back, a spiral, blackened-iron staircase wound up through a round hole in the ceiling. On the stairs stood a gnarled, hunched-over man wearing a green robe. His hands were curled around a long, wooden staff almost as gnarled as he. A narrow, purple bruise crossed his forehead. He was smiling, showing the few yellow and black teeth left in his head.

In front of the robed man stood five more black-clad cultists, each carrying a battle axe at the ready. The moment the door burst open, the soldiers bolted forward. Metal rang on metal as Whitman and Clemf took the charge.

Tasca's bow twanged, and his arrow shot over the heads of the advancing soldiers, winging through the air toward the gnarled man. It struck its mark, piercing the man in his breast. As soon as the projectile hit, however, it vanished, seeming to disappear without any fanfare into thin air.

The robed man rubbed his twisted fingers over the polished surface of his staff. He seemed to be caressing the gnarled length of wood with as much care and attention as he might lavish on a beautiful woman. Looking down at the group from his perch on the spiraling stairs, he pointed the head of the staff at Tasca and nodded once, whispering something into the air. A ghostly white pair of magical manacles shot out, tracing back along the exact path traveled by the elf's arrow.

Tasca shrieked as the magical energies bore down on him. He tried to dodge the spell, but it was no use. The manacles encased his entire body, flaring once when they hit before disappearing. The elf took one more step, then froze in place, eternally dodging away from a spell that he couldn't escape.

Whitman's hammer connected with a cultist's helm, making a satisfying sound like a bell tolling. The man's head flopped back across his shoulders on his broken neck, looking almost like a turtle retreating into its shell.

The four remaining men swung their battle axes. Whitman blocked one with a well-placed hammer blow, but a second got past his defenses. The blade bit into his beard. A long strand of graying hair flopped to the ground with a thin line of blood rimming the outside edge.

The other two men attacked Clemf. Their blades swung in at the same time, one high, one low. Clemf leaned away from the strikes by arching his back and pulling his chest away from the higher of the two axes. The razor-sharp edge whispered past his chestplate, barely missing.

With a desperate, off-balance swing of his sword, Clemf swung at the low weapon. His longsword whistled down and crashed into the hilt of the battle axe. Metal bit into wood, and Clemf's blow managed to push the soldier's attack off target. The second blade kissed the edge of his shin, slicing into the leather bands that held his armor in place. The long, metal plate that protected his lower leg dropped to the floor with a clatter.

The attacker twisted his wrists and yanked back on his weapon. Clemf's sword, still stuck in the wooden shaft of the battle axe, came free of his hands, and he stumbled forward offbalance.

Regdar watched Clemf lose his blade and then his balance. Not wasting any time, the big fighter leaped over the tattooed man's bent-over frame, greatsword held high over his head. With a savage cry, Regdar smashed his blade down on the soldier's shoulder. The magical blade beamed brightly for a brief moment as it sliced through metal, leather, flesh, and bone. The soldier screamed, and his arm dropped to the ground with a clatter. Blood from the freshly opened wound spilled out over his severed arm, his battle axe, and Clemf's sword still embedded in its handle.

Regdar let go of his sword with one hand and jammed his fingers into the other soldier's helm. Slipping through the eye slit, his extended digits poked the soldier in his right eye. Regdar felt something soft and slippery at the tip of his metal gauntlet. With a vicious jab, he thrust his hand farther into the helmet. The soldier screamed and stumbled back, streaming blood and viscous matter from his faceplate.

Clemf got to his feet and scrounged for his sword. He shoved the armless man to the ground and then spied his weapon, now covered in blood. He snatched it up and rose to his full height in the middle of the room, sword in hand.

The gnarled man on the stairs looked down from his perch at the tattooed fighter. Narrowing his gaze, he wiggled his fingers in the air, ending with a shout and several jerking motions with his wrist.

Regdar watched as Clemf's knees shook and his shoulders slumped. He dropped the sword he had just picked up, and he let out a scream that made the tiny hairs on the small of Regdar's back stand on end. Then Clemf turned and bolted from the room, pushing past the immobile elf and crashing haphazardly into the doorframe on his way out.

Whitman hefted his hammer and struck with a bone crunching blow.

"That's for my beard," he shouted.

The soldier before him shook from the blow. He'd managed to block the mighty weapon from striking him, but the shock of the impact vibrated through his body. The dwarf wound up and struck again. This time he managed to slip past the soldier's axe and hit him on the forearm, knocking the weapon from his grasp. Whitman rolled the momentum of his swing into another, follow-through attack. The third blow hit the same forearm with a distinct popping sound.

Though he was grievously injured, the black-armored minion still stood, and he pulled a dagger from its sheath with his good hand. His injured arm swung loosely at his side as he crouched, holding the blade out before him, taking short steps away from the ornery dwarf.

"That's right," shouted the dwarf. "Be afraid. Be very afraid."

The only uninjured soldier remaining took one look at the angry dwarf and turned his attention on Regdar. Winding up as if he were chopping wood, he bent his knees and swung his axe down, meaning to split the big fighter in two. Regdar swiped his blade up with both hands. The two weapons collided with a gut-wrenching clang, and sparks flew in the air. Both men were knocked back by the impact. Regdar sighted down his blade, never before having seen fireworks issue from his weapon.

The greatsword was untarnished, its shiny finish still polished and bright. The soldier's axe, however, was a different story. The impact with Regdar's magical sword took a huge bite out of the axe. If he hadn't known better, Regdar might have thought the soldier's weapon had been some monster's afternoon snack.

The armless soldier still lay on the floor, unmoving, where Clemf had knocked him. His counterpart still struggled with his ruined eye. He had removed his gauntlets and now was gently probing the gory hole in his face where his eye had been.

Regdar lunged at the uninjured soldier. Feigning to the left, he drew out the man's parry and changed directions at the last second. The edge of his blade slipped past the notched head of the man's axe, expertly angling between metal plates to strike home. The big fighter pushed the blade deep into the soldier's chest.

Regdar held tightly to the hilt of his greatsword and twisted the weapon in the wound. The big fighter then wrenched it out and watched the soldier slump to the floor.

The robed mage eyed the two remaining intruders. Shifting his glare from Whitman to Regdar and back again, the gnarled old man began reciting another spell.

Regdar saw the green-robed man, his eyes closed, sprinkle dust into the air. A large, brilliantly blue magical cloud appeared, obscuring the gnarled man from view. The cloud drifted across the open room and sank to the floor, where it surrounded the dwarf.

The soldier with the dagger and broken arm backed away from Whitman, taking advantage of the spell to open the distance between him and the dwarf. Retreating all the way to the far wall, the man braced himself, holding his puny weapon menacingly before him.

Whitman was completely gone from view. Tasca was frozen solid, holding the same pose that he had through the entire encounter. Clemf was nowhere to be seen, fleeing in panic.

With a loud shout, Regdar charged across the room toward the wizard. Though the fighter was strong and quite fast, his heavy armor slowed him down enough for the spellcaster to begin chanting the words of another spell. His stubby fingers wiggled at the oncoming fighter.

Halfway across the floor, Regdar realized that he wouldn't be able to reach the gnarled, old man before he could cast the magic already forming on his lips. Twirling his sword overhead, Regdar pointed the tip of the blade at the stairs, planted his front foot, and hurled his magical greatsword like a javelin.

The well-made weapon hung in midair for a brief moment. Though the blacksmith who crafted it never intended it for throwing, the blade carved a perfect arc as it plunged away from Regdar's hand. Its tip descended, and the magically sharpened sword pierced the hood of the green robe, then clanked as it hit the stair behind the wizard.

Regdar stumbled forward, trying to catch his balance. He looked up at the spellcaster, bracing himself for whatever magical malady or monstrosity was about to strike him. The old man raised his hands, his eyes glaring down at the fighter.

Then he gasped and reached for his throat. Blood flowed out through his fingers as he clasped them tightly around his neck. The spell he had been forming slipped from his lips and was gone. His attention turned to stopping the flow of blood from the tremendous sword wound in his neck.

Regdar charged the stairs once again. When he reached the old man, he grabbed him by the front of his garment and hefted him over the railing, pulling him down to the floor and smashing his face against the stone tiles. The impact knocked the old wizard's head sideways, tearing the wound in his neck open further. Blood rushed out, and the spellcaster's body shuddered once, then fell still.

Leaving the gnarled old man in a heap on the ground, Regdar retrieved his sword and took a look around. The cloud surrounding Whitman was gone, and the dwarf lay on the floor, obviously breathing but otherwise unmoving. Tasca remained stationary, and Clemf hadn't returned.

Regdar turned his attention to the two living but badly injured soldiers. The man whose eye Regdar had gouged out had fallen to the floor. His face lay in a puddle of his own blood and vomit, and blood continued pumping from his ruined eye socket. The other man still stood with his back against the wall. He had removed his helm, and his face was a ghostly white. The arm Whitman had smashed was tremendously swollen, and the man was obviously in a lot of pain. Sweat rolled down his forehead, and he had a hard time keeping his dagger pointed out in front of him.

The injured soldier shook his head, trying to focus his eyes on Regdar. He struggled to keep them from rolling back in his head.

Regdar took a couple of steps toward the man. "I don't suppose you're going to tell me what you know about Lindroos and her plans for New Koratia."

The cultist steeled himself and thrust his dagger out toward Regdar as far as he could.

"Come on now," coaxed the big fighter. "I don't want to kill you." He lowered his sword and began fishing around inside his backpack. "Tell me what she wants with Naull and what evil she's up to, and I'll take care of that wound for you." He pulled a pearly, opalescent flask from his bag and shook it. The liquid inside made a satisfying sloshing sound.

The soldier looked at the flask with wide eyes. He turned to Regdar, lifted the dagger to his own chin, and plunged it into his throat. A rush of blood spilled to the floor, and the cultist collapsed beside it.

Regdar rushed over to Whitman. The dwarf lay on his side, breathing easily, his lips flapping a bit as they let out a breath of air, a small drip of drool running down the side of his face. The human grabbed his prone friend by the shoulder, and Whitman let out a long, snorting breath.

"Huh?" Whitman shook his head and rolled to his side, startled alert.

"Are you all right?" asked Regdar.

Whitman wiped the drool from his beard and sat up. He looked up at the big man and nodded.

Regdar slapped him on the arm and went to check on Tasca. The elf still stood frozen in place, his eyes moving side to side, alert but unmoving. Regdar tried to shake him as he had the dwarf, but it did no good. Tasca remained magically stuck, as if a statue.

While Regdar examined the elf, Clemf returned. He had a sheepish look on his face, and he poked his head around, surveying the room.

"They're all dead or dying," said Regdar, standing up straight. "You okay?"

Clemf straightened up and nodded hesitantly. "Yeah." He pointed to the dead wizard with his chin. "You kill him?"

Regdar nodded.

Clemf looked to the floor. "Good."

Soon Tasca's rigid form began to soften, and he slowly stood up straight as the spell expired.

He rubbed his neck. "Damn. I hate it when that happens."

Whitman led the way up the spiral stairs, and they reached the top without incident. The floor spread out in a small, square room around the hole where the stairs entered from below. There was one torch on each of three walls and a door in the third.

"Kick, kill, take," said Whitman, gently probing the smooth spot where his beard had been partially cut from his face.

Tasca and Regdar nocked arrows to their bows. Clemf stood beside the dwarf, sword at the ready.

Whitman looked at the other three men, nodded, then took two running steps forward, lifting his leg and kicking the door near the handle with a powerful thrust.

The door creaked open, resisting Whitman's forceful entry but giving way all the same. Inside, the room was filled with natural light. The wall opposite the door was made of a series of pillars and arches. The space between the stone supports was open to the outside. The walls to the east and west were solid stone like those the group had encountered below. Unlike the rest of the fortress however, the floor was made from slatted wooden panels. Many, many feet had passed over these boards, wearing them thin in places and leaving the floor smooth and shiny.

In the middle of the room, backlit by the light coming in from the overcast sky, stood a petite figure, hands grasped tightly around something, face pointing toward the floor.

Regdar pulled his arrow tight against his bow string, then relaxed.

"Naull," he said with enough inflection to make it sound somewhere between a question and a summons.

The figure didn't look up.

The men entered through the open door and spread out. Tasca looked at Regdar, holding his bow taught.

The big fighter shook his head. "It's her," he said. He lowered his bow and crossed the floor.

"Naull," he said again, this time a little louder. "Naull, it's me, Regdar."

Naull looked up from the floor. Her mouth moved, and she was whispering something Regdar could not hear. In her hands she held a partially unraveled scroll. The arcane markings on the rolled vellum flared and disappeared, and Naull's lips stopped moving, curling up into a smile.

The light pouring into the room wavered then disappeared. The gray, overcast sky slipped away, replaced by speckled black stone. Torches flickered along the walls, illuminating the outlines of a dozen or more black-clad soldiers. All of them held longswords at the ready, and they surrounded the four fighters.

Lindroos stepped out next to Naull, accompanied by four bald, burly men with purple vests and scimitars tucked into orange sashes at their waists. They were all quite large and resembled the efreeti Regdar and company had bested on the lower level.

"Hello, Regdar," said Lindroos with a smile. "It's time you met my companions. This is Shirzad—" she pointed to one of the burley men and continued around—"Parviz, Hebola, and Tam."

The four burly men each bowed.

"They are jann from the court of Vizier Haleh," explained the blackguard. Then she turned to Naull. The fallen paladin ran her finger along the slight wizard's cheek, caressing her skin. "You already know my close friend Naull."

Regdar dropped his bow to the floor and pulled his greatsword from its sheath. His heart pounded in his chest, and the skin on the back of his neck tingled where the hairs stood on end.

He squeezed the hilt of his sword. "What is it you want from me, Lindroos?"

"I want what I've always wanted of you and those of your kind," she said, pacing closer to the big fighter. "I want all of you to die."

The room broke out in fighting. Black-clad soldiers charged in at the group of four intruders in a rush of metal and blades.

Whitman's hammer pounded out a staccato rhythm against two soldiers' banded-mail armor. Attack then parry. Attack then parry. The dwarf whirled and struck, defending himself with long, sweeping arcs of his hammer, then smashing down on his opponent with a tremendous blow.

Clemf batted away blades as fast as they came at him. He jabbed back at one soldier, catching him in the throat and sending him back a step. Though he managed to wound his opponent, the lunge cost him. Another soldier slashed at Clemf's exposed ribs, opening a small wound across his stomach and down toward his groin. The tattooed human growled at his attacker and spun on him. His breathing became deep and his chest rose and fell as if he were an angry bull. With a powerful wail, Clemf stepped forward and beheaded two soldiers with one swing of his longsword.

Tasca fired arrows into the approaching crowd of swordsmen at a furious pace. His fingers flew over the bow string, releasing two arrows at a time and reloading in the blink of an eye. Nearly every arrow he fired found its mark, but his attacks didn't stop the soldiers from advancing. Eventually he had to drop his bow and draw his rapier. With swashbuckling flare, the roguish elf battled his adversaries, trading blows even when he was surrounded and flanked.

Regdar stepped forward and grabbed Naull by the arm.

"Naull!" he shouted. "Naull, don't you remember me?"

The slight wizard pulled away from his grip and glared up at him with narrowed eyes.

"I remember you," she said, hatred dripping from her words. "You left me to die." She spat in his face then bent down to pick up a quarterstaff lying on the ground near her feet.

"That's not tru—"

His words were cut off by a hard crack to his ribs. Gasping to regain his lost breath, the big fighter took a step back as Naull bent into a crouch, twirling her quarterstaff for another strike.

"Naull," he pleaded. "What are you doing? You must remember I didn't want to leave you." He held his arms out to his sides, trying to look less menacing.

"That's not how I remember it," she said, hurling the head of her staff at Regdar.

The fighter dodged back, narrowly avoiding the blow.

"But . . . but, you asked me to leave," he said.

His words were again cut short by another whizzing attack.

This time Regdar had to use his greatsword to block. The enchanted blade bit into the dense wood of the staff, and Naull struggled to free her weapon. That left her ribs exposed to a counter strike. Regdar took note but stayed his blade.

Emitting a frustrated, scratchy cry, the slight wizard gave her staff a great tug, pulling it free. She took a step back, straightened her robes, and caught her breath.

"Why would I ask you to leave?" she shouted from two long paces away. "Surely a big, strong fighter like you could have protected a frail little wizard like me."

Regdar wrinkled his forehead, confused. "It was you who saved me that day." The memory of being pulled by Alhandra and Krusk from the City of Fire as it shifted into the Elemental Plane of Fire ran through his head. "When I had to leave you there, injured and trapped with that bitch Lindroos—" he lowered his gaze, and his lip curled up at the edge—"something inside me died." He took a step forward.

"How very sweet." Naull charged forward, her quarterstaff lowered like a lance.

She got a good jump and caught Regdar off guard. The heavy staff plunged into Regdar's stomach where the efreeti's falchion had split his breastplate. He twisted to one side, defending his midsection with a snap reaction borne of long campaigns in the bowels of dank, decrepit dungeons. The big fighter's greatsword swept around in a blinding arc, spanking away the quarterstaff. His gauntleted hand came around as well, connecting with the petite wizard's chin and knocking her to the ground with a single blow.

Naull landed on her back with a surprised grunt. A trickle of blood ran from her split lower lip, and she held her eyes shut, grimacing from pain.

Regdar stepped back. He looked down on Naull, feeling pangs of guilt. He started to kneel next to her. More than anything he wanted to cradle her in his arms, to tell her how sorry he was—to tell her about the gaping hole in his chest that had been punched there when he left her in the City of Fire.

But he hesitated.

Turning around, he took in the terrible battle unfolding around his companions. Whitman, Tasca, and Clemf stood back to back to back, surrounded by half a dozen cultist soldiers and four jann. Lindroos stood to one side, watching and smiling at the obvious advantage she enjoyed.

Whitman struck down another soldier with a hammer blow that might have felled a hill giant. Regdar turned away, hoping his men could hold there own for a moment longer, while he decided what to do with Naull.

Jozan stepped through the hallowed arches of St. Clembert's cathedral. He paused to admire the beautiful architecture. The carved stone pillars on each side depicted scenes of terrible carnage—demons flooding across a huge plain and crashing into a line of mighty paladins. At the head of the holy warriors stood a protector from the heavens. Though he was only a man, he stood a full head taller than all the rest. His sword rose high above the swarming masses, and his armor gleamed with a holy light. His eyes looked out at the advancing hordes, concentrating but unafraid. He held his chest out as he strode forward into a pack of fanged demons, each intent on devouring the man whole.

"I see you're familiar with this cathedral's namesake," said a woman's voice.

Jozan turned around to see a tall, hard-looking woman in gleaming plate armor. He smiled.

"Alhandra," he said. "Blessings be with you."

"And also with you," she replied, smiling back. "Do you know the story of how the paladin Clembert became a saint?" she asked, nodding toward the sculpted pillar.

Jozan scratched his chin. "No, actually, I'm not sure I do."

Alhandra grabbed his elbow and spun him around. She pointed at the demons. "Thousands of years ago, a demon lord by the name of Jalie Squarefoot managed to convince a band of adventurers to travel to the third layer of Hell. Once there, the dim-witted fools were tricked into starting the legendary Doom Clock." She moved her finger along the formed stone, rubbing it across demon horns and coming to rest on top of a deep chasm at the back of the evil horde.

"Once the clock came out of its millennia-long slumber, it began unraveling the fibers of time." She looked at Jozan. "The clock actually had the power to pull apart the fabric that separates the planes." She looked back to the battle scene. "As it moved from the third layer of Hell to the ninth, the huge, six-legged structure collected behind it a veritable army of crazed demons all wanting to wreak havoc on the other planes. Once it reached the ninth layer, it opened a portal to this world." Alhandra ran her hand back across the entire, grisly scene.

"Here it unleashed the chaos army you see depicted onto our land." Taking a step around the pillar, the paladin admired the tall, determined man at the head of the holy army. "The great paladin Clembert gathered to him the mightiest army of paladins and holy men ever to fight together on this plane." The paladin shrugged. "Or any other for that matter."

Alhandra let out a heavy sigh. "Many good, righteous men and women died that day." She touched the sculpture of the heroic man. "Including the paladin Clembert. But his loss was not in vain. His efforts and those of the people who followed him saved our world from being overrun by the evil horde. If it hadn't been for them, this world would be nothing more than the tenth plane of Hell."

"Then the church sainted Clembert for his bravery and service to Pelor?" prompted Jozan.

Alhandra nodded. "Yes, but not for many centuries." She sighed again. "You see, at that time, the elders decided that if the general population knew how close they had come to being enslaved by the dark forces of evil, it might shake their faith in the church. Even though Clembert's bravery and sacrifice saved our world, the church set out to intentionally cover up all details of the demon invasion." She turned and looked at Jozan. "The name Clembert was erased from all church documents, and his loyal service to Pelor went completely unrecognized by the establishment."

"But not unrecognized by Pelor," said Jozan.

Alhandra smiled. "Your faith is stronger than when last we met, cleric. It's good to see."

Jozan blushed. "Experience has a way of clearing up the quandaries of youth."

Alhandra stepped away from the pillar. She waved to Jozan. "Come," she said.

The two walked through the courtyard of the cathedral.

"Tell me," said the paladin as they strolled, "what brings you to St. Clembert's?"

"Actually," replied the cleric, "my business here is done. I was on my way out when you found me."

The paladin nodded. "Any news of our mutual friends?"

Jozan whistled. "Too much to tell in one afternoon," he said. "I'll see if I can't give you the condensed version."

"You do that." Alhandra chuckled. "I wouldn't want to keep you here any longer than need be."

Jozan blushed. "You misunderstand."

Alhandra put her hand on his shoulder. "Go on, I'm only joking."

Jozan blushed more deeply at her touch, then he looked away. "Well, last I saw Lidda, she was up to her usual antics. She convinced Krusk to head over to New Coast for one of her 'entrepreneurial ventures.'"

They both laughed.

"I haven't seen them since they left, but knowing Lidda, they're likely in jail, or breaking out of jail, or getting someone killed," continued the cleric.

"Perhaps all three," agreed Alhandra.

"I passed through New Koratia to see Regdar on my way here."

The paladin wrinkled her forehead. "New Koratia? That's not exactly on the way to St. Clembert's unless you're coming from the middle of the ocean."

Jozan nodded. "You're right," he admitted, "but I had news about Naull."

Alhandra stopped dead in her tracks. "Naull?"

"Yes." Jozan stopped as well. "I met some missionaries who had barely escaped a run-in with a slave caravan," he explained. "One of them used to deliver apples to Naull's mentor, so he knew Naull's face. He recognized her in the caravan." The cleric shrugged. "I thought Regdar should know. He's been almost suicidal ever since he lost her."

Alhandra stood in the courtyard of St. Clembert's, her jaw rigid, her gaze pointed toward the sky.

Jozan looked at her from the corner of his eye. "Alhandra, what is it?"

The paladin lowered her stare, and her eyes pierced straight through Jozan, giving him an uneasy feeling.

"Are you sure this man was telling the truth?"

The cleric nodded. "I even prayed to Pelor for guidance." He looked up. "I believe what he said was true."

"And you told Regdar all of this?"

Jozan nodded. "Yes. Why?"

Alhandra shook her head. "Because if Naull is alive, then so too may be my sister—the blackguard Lindroos."

A cold chill ran down Jozan's spine. "Regdar went to find Naull," he said.

"When he finds her," Alhandra finished the cleric's thought, "he'll find Lindroos."

Jozan stood motionless for a moment.

"We've got to help him," said Alhandra.

Jozan shook himself out of his brief stupor. "But he went to Mt. Fear. That's more than a week's travel by foot, four days even by horse. He could be dead by then."

"Come with me." Alhandra jogged off across the courtyard. "I know someone who might be of help."

Regdar waved his hands in front of him, hoping to ward off what was coming. "Naull, can't we just talk about this?"

The petite wizard smiled as she recited the last few words of her spell—a spell Regdar had heard too many times in his career as a soldier. As she finished the incantation, three swirling balls of purple-blue energy appeared in her hand. She eyed them briefly, then turned her attention to Regdar, a satisfied, cocky look on her face.

"You men are all alike," she said.

The first of the magical missiles launched from her palm and struck Regdar in the middle of the chest. He hissed air in through his gritted teeth.

"You always want a second chance," continued the wizard. She jutted her hand out, and the second ball corkscrewed at blinding speed, slamming into Regdar's arm.

"Oww!" Regdar shouted. He shook his hand and wrist as if he'd just hit his thumb with a builder's hammer.

Naull paid him no mind. "Always want to talk about things after the deeds are done, as if that can take away the pain and the humiliation. Never think about how a woman might feel before you hurt her." Naull launched the last missile.

The magical energy once again slammed Regdar and dissipated over his body, sparking and arcing across the seams in his armor.

The big fighter staggered back, off balance from the impact of Naull's magical onslaught. "Please, Naull, I know you're upset, but what you're doing isn't right. Will you please just wait a second?"

Naull raised her hands again, preparing another spell. "Wait? Like you waited for me in the City of Fire?" she screamed.

Regdar's face flushed red. "Had I known—"

"I don't want to hear your excuses." She began chanting the words of the spell.

Regdar lunged forward and grabbed Naull's arm. He caught hold of her wrist and twisted it, turning her around and pinning her bent arm behind her back. Naull screeched like a harpy and tried to pull away. Her spell was ruined, the words of her incantation unfinished.

"Let go of me, you dim-witted troglodyte." The petite wizard flailed, wrenching her arm back and forth as she tried to struggle free.

Regdar felt her shoulder pull tight, then pop. "You're going to hurt yourself."

Naull spun her head around and glared at the big fighter. "You're the one holding my arm." She let her knees collapse and screamed at the top of her lungs, "You broke it! You broke my arm!"

Naull's cries of pain reminded Regdar of the sounds goblins make when they're being eaten alive by spiders. He let go of her.

The wizard pulled her injured arm up against her chest and rolled onto her side in a fetal ball, where she began to sob.

Regdar looked down on her, his chest constricted with guilt. He felt like a parent who had accidentally injured a child in anger, a moment of unthinking anger that could never be retracted or made right. He bent over Naull.

"Dear Pelor," he said. "Please, Naull, forgive me. I didn't mean to—"

Naull rolled onto her back and reached up between the big fighter's legs. Grabbing hold of his crotch, she shouted an arcane word, and a flood of magical energy coursed out of her fingertips.

As the spell's power flowed into the staggered fighter, Naull smiled up at him.

"Can you see your god now?" she asked. "Tell him you'll be along shortly."

Regdar couldn't move. He was pinned in place by the most excruciating pain imaginable. He couldn't move, couldn't even scream. He'd been told by veteran soldiers that being stabbed in the kidney was the worst, most paralyzingly painful way to kill a man, but those old warriors were wrong. The muscles of his groin twitched and constricted, felt as if they were on fire, as if they were being burned, electrocuted, and torn away by dull claws at the same time. He was sure he lost control of his bladder.

When the spell ended and the arcane pain stopped flowing, Regdar staggered backward. The pain had numbed his mind, his head buzzed with a mixture of relief and horror.

Naull rubbed her arm. It was obviously not broken. Slowly the wizard rose to her feet, a sly smile playing on her lips.

Regdar groaned. He had never really wanted to be a father, but he now felt certain that that option was no longer available to him. Taking a deep breath and shaking his head to clear the fog.

Pulling back his gauntleted hand, he made a fist. "I've had enough," he said.

The metal of his gauntlet rang against the bones in the wizard's face. A big, red blotch appeared on Naull's forehead as she reeled backward, and blood gushed from her nose. The wizard rocked on her heals for a moment, then her eyes rolled back in her head, and she fell, landing hard on the wooden floor with a loud thud.

Regdar looked down at the crumpled form of the woman he loved. "Even I have my limit," he said, then he turned around to join the fray.

Behind Regdar, in the middle of the room, the fighting came to a sudden stop. The few remaining soldiers formed a tight ring around Whitman, Tasca, and Clemf. They held their swords out menacingly, jabbing at the dwarf, elf, and human in the center.

The four jann stood behind the soldiers, making a second ring around the trapped fighters. They leered at the men in the middle.

Lindroos reclined against the nearest wall, smiling. "Well, Regdar," said the blackguard, "it looks as if I win."

Regdar gripped the hilt of his magical greatsword. "How do you figure?"

"Consider the situation," said Lindroos, standing up from her comfortable position on the wall. "Your friends are completely surrounded, and you are outnumbered more than two to one," she said. "I never was good at math, but still, I think that means I have the advantage."

Regdar looked at Lindroos for a moment. First she kills Naull, he thought, then she returns as Naull's lover. The big fighter narrowed his eyes.

"You aren't good at numbers," he replied.

Regdar took three huge, running steps forward, charging the blackguard in a sudden rush. With practiced flair, the veteran fighter swung his greatsword up and around in a blinding arc. Lindroos's eyes flew wide, and she barely managed to get her jet black blade up in time to keep Regdar from taking her head off at the neck.

The attack had caught her off guard, and her minions momentarily turned their attention from the three fighters they surrounded to the crazed human charging their leader. That was all the opening that the trapped trio needed.

Whitman shoved the soldier in front of him. The man lost his balance and fell backward. The dwarf's hammer struck down within a blink and clanged against splintmail. The downed soldier let out a strangled groan as his ribcage collapsed and broken bone ends pierced his lungs.

The janni behind the soldier stepped forward onto the dying soldier's chest, adding to his agony. Clemf lunged into the hole and jammed the tip of his longsword into the janni's ribs. The outsider shrieked and leaped straight up into the air, where it flew to the ceiling and out of sword reach.

Tasca also took advantage of the sudden distraction and gap in the enemy ring. The spry elf bent his knees and sprang forward, launching himself like a ballista bolt through the hole. Two soldiers and two jann swiped at him as he soared by, but all of them missed, unable to keep up with the speedy elf.

Lindroos retained her composure as she traded blows with Regdar.

"You can't beat me," she taunted, lunging forward and barely missing Regdar's chin.

"Oh no?" countered the big fighter. "What makes you so sure?"

Lindroos smiled. "Them," she said, pointing behind Regdar.

Regdar chuckled without humor. "You don't expect me to fall for that stupid trick, do you?"

Lindroos stepped back, completely disengaging from their fight. "Oh, no," she said. "Look for yourself."

The sound of marching feet drew Regdar's glance back over his shoulder. Coming through the door that Whitman had kicked in was another squad of Lindroos's black-clad soldiers—perhaps two dozen or more in all.

"Like I said," taunted the blackguard, "I never was good at math. I guess I made a mistake when I said you were outnumbered two to one."

Regdar turned and charged toward the new arrivals, hoping he could bottleneck them in the narrow doorframe. His blade swooped down to split a soldier's head, but it bounced away, blocked by a pair of crossed longswords. Pulling back, Regdar barely managed to evade several counterattacks. The tip of one blade caught him on the elbow but failed to find the gap in his armor's joint.

"The luck of Pelor," he said, and he waded in.

Whitman gritted his teeth. In three successive hammer blows, he'd managed to take three soldiers out of the fight. Only one of them was dead, but even if the others recovered their wits in short order, it was three blades he didn't need to deal with right at this moment. The jann were another problem entirely. Clemf had forced one to take flight, but the other three had their scimitars out, and they were looking for blood.

Whitman heard a high-pitched whistle. The sound made the skin along his spine crawl. He'd heard that noise before, and he knew what it meant—duck! Rolling into a ball, the dwarf tumbled forward. He could feel a slight breeze rush by as a scimitar sliced the air where he had been standing only a moment before.

Getting to his feet, Whitman turned to face the janni and its curved blade. The bare-chested outsider had a look of contempt on its face, and it turned the blade around for another attack.

"Let me guess," said Whitman, "you're Tweedledum?"

The janni sneered and swung its blade. Whitman nearly tripped over one of the downed soldiers as he dodged away.

"I am called Shirzad," said the janni. "I tell you this so you will know who to fear in the afterlife."

The dwarf regained his full balance, and he glared back, gripping his hammer tightly with both hands. "And I am called Whitman," replied the dwarf. "I tell you this so mine will be the last name you hear in this world." Whitman swept his magical weapon behind him then up over his head. With tremendous force, the dwarf slammed down the hammer with all his might. It struck the janni's sword and bashed it aside without slowing, then continued on into the outsider's chest. The blow lifted Whitman from his feet, and a tremendous crack echoed across the room.

The janni's knees buckled, and its eyes rolled back into its head. The exposed flesh on its naked chest rippled in waves like liquid as the sound jolted through the huge body. The outsider convulsed once again and vomited soupy, green liquid.

"Damn," shouted the dwarf.

The janni collapsed forward to the floor, falling so that its forehead hit the ground with a great thump.

Whitman heard the high-pitched whistle too late this time. He screamed as searing pain erupted along his back. He spun around to see the other two jann behind him. One held a scimitar tipped in blood. The other swung its curved blade, obviously intending to take Whitman's head as a trophy. The dwarf ducked, but the pain in his back slowed his reaction so that the blade connected with his helm, knocking it off. A heavy, ringing sound bounced back and forth between his ears, and his vision went blurry. He knew there were only two jann standing before him, but he could have sworn there were four.

His vision cleared quickly, but Whitman was momentarily unsure. He now saw three jann around him. He realized that the third, which had been flying near the ceiling, must have landed behind him, trapping the dwarf between all three outsiders.

"This isn't good."

One of the jann snapped its fingers, and in a blink all of them disappeared from view.

"Oh, this really isn't good."

Tasca backed himself into the corner and fired arrows into the fray as fast and as hard as he could. The metal arrowheads made satisfying pinging sounds as they punctured splintmail, and the screams of the men as they were shot was even more reassuring.

Despite Regdar's heroic stand at the door, the room was filling quickly with more soldiers. Whitman was surrounded by jann, and Tasca couldn't see Clemf anywhere. He fired two arrows at once. A soldier shrieked as both projectiles penetrated his chest, but he didn't fall.

"That'll be all out of you," came a voice from Tasca's left.

The elf ducked, an instinctive reaction to being startled in battle. A thick black blade sparked as it hit the stone wall. Chips of broken brick rained down on the crouched elf's head.

Dropping his bow, Tasca somersaulted away from the wall so that he landed on his feet, his rapier in hand. He looked up into the face of the blackguard.

"I'm going to enjoy this," she said. Then she charged.

Tasca braced himself, watching the tip of the long, black blade as it zigzagged toward him.

Lindroos feinted left and changed direction. Tasca weaved his blade through the air, following the move with an expert eye. The blackguard grunted and leaned into her strike. Her blade pushed hard against the elf's rapier, sliding down its length with a long grinding noise.

Tasca pushed back with all of his strength, but the blackguard simply overpowered him. Time seemed to slow down as the black blade slid closer and closer to his face. The sounds of battle fell away, leaving only the *shing* of metal on metal. Tasca gave ground, dodging away in a complete retreat.

Too late.

Lindroos's blade slipped past his guard and caught the elf on the cheek, opening a deep wound across his face. Tasca hissed and jerked backward, slamming into the wall.

"Too bad," taunted the blackguard. "It's a shame to cut up such a pretty face."

Clemf fought for his life, surrounded by a dozen cultist soldiers.

"Out of the cook pot into the campfire," he said, bashing away attacks one after the other. His efforts were focused exclusively on defending himself. He didn't have time to counterattack or even think about how he was going to get out of this mess.

Another longsword came at his head. Clemf ducked. A second came in at his knees. He slapped it aside with his blade. A third jabbed at his ribs. It glanced off his armor.

A sharp pain shot through the back of his right leg. Clemf howled and pulled himself away, stumbling headlong into two soldiers. The change was unintentional, but the unexpected movement knocked several of Clemf's attackers backward.

The tattooed warrior got tangled up in the pile of flailing bodies. He put out his hand to catch himself. From out of nowhere, a heavy boot caught him in the chest. He dropped his longsword and fell to his knees.

Panting, resting on all fours, Clemf looked down at the wooden slats that made up the flooring. Though he felt no pain, he could see drips of blood falling from his body. They made a slight tapping sound as they impacted the floor.

He wondered at the noise. So odd that amid all the clanging, smashing, fighting, and dying that he could hear the drops of blood. For a moment, all that existed in the room was the wooden floor and the ever-changing crimson patterns forming and reforming with each splash.

The unmistakable sound of metal straining then failing rang though Clemf's ears, followed by a hollow noise like a melon being dropped on a hard stone floor. Clemf watched as the drips of blood grew larger, then turned into a steady stream. The deluge hit the ground and splashed, throwing out more drips in a circular pattern.

"How beautiful," said the tattooed human.

Clemf collapsed to the floor, facedown in a pool of blood.

Regdar's stalling tactic didn't work for long. The narrow door-frame made a good bottleneck, but the fight pitted one man against two dozen. Even a veteran fighter like Regdar couldn't expect to hold them forever.

The front line pushed back against Regdar's assault, and the soldiers in the rear slipped inside the door, working their way past the big fighter and into battle with the other three. In moments, Regdar was again surrounded, and so were his friends.

Regdar slashed his greatsword across one soldier, slicing through the protective metal around his neck and cleaving into the flesh and bone beneath. The man let out a cry and stumbled back. Regdar followed through, taking the opportunity to step out from between the men surrounding him. Spinning, he put his back against the wall to protect his flank.

As he turned around, he got a view of the entire room. Before him stood three cultists ready for a fight. Behind them, Whitman was surrounded by three jann. In the corner, Tasca was locked in combat with Lindroos, his face bleeding from a long wound.

Then he saw Clemf, outnumbered ten to one, fall to his hands and knees. Before Regdar could move or even speak, a huge soldier raised his sword overhead with the tip pointing straight down, right at where Clemf had fallen. Regdar's blood ran cold, and a numbing tingle ran down his spine.

The soldier's arms stabbed down.

The sound of armor complaining as it was punctured followed, and Regdar felt his heart slip into his stomach.

The ring of soldiers surrounding Clemf turned away and broke up, heading for the other three fighters. With his back against the wall, Regdar fought off three attackers of his own. More were on their way. As the center of the room cleared, Regdar's worst fears were proven. Clemf lay facedown on the floor in a growing pool of blood.

Regdar's lip curled. He made eye contact with each of the three men standing before him.

"I'm going to kill you," he said through gritted teeth. "If I have to come back from the grave to do it, I'll kill *all* of you." His greatsword caught the first soldier between the ribs. The magical blade bit deep, and the man's eyes rolled back in his head as he fell dead.

Regdar pulled out the blade, savoring the sight of blood running down its length. He lunged at the second soldier, but the blow was parried. The man bashed Regdar's sword against the wall and pinned it there with the flat of his own blade.

Regdar struggled to free his weapon, but he couldn't get enough leverage. With his back against the wall and his arm held fast, his chest and belly were completely exposed. The third cultist saw the opening and sliced down. His razor-sharp weapon slipped between the plates in Regdar's armor.

A burning sensation blossomed on Regdar's left shoulder, and he could feel his warm blood seep into his armpit and run down his ribs. With his back against the wall, he couldn't pull back, so instead he jerked sideways, dislodging the blade but not before the weapon tore a much larger gash in his hide.

Regdar drew in a sharp breath between gritted teeth, making a hissing sound as he did. The wound the soldier had opened was deep, and it hurt. To make matters worse, a new group of soldiers had surrounded the big fighter. The cultists lined up in a semicircle, three rows deep, waiting their turn to take their best shot at Captain Regdar.

A pop, as loud as a cannon shot, echoed off the black stone walls, startling everyone. In the far corner, filling the only unpopulated section of the large room, a softly glowing circle of blue-white faded into view. A cylinder of magical light grew from the circle, rising from the floor to the ceiling. The light pulsed once, and the glow began to fade. In its place, several figures took shape.

"Lindroos," came a woman's voice from inside the cylinder, "whatever evil scheme you're plotting comes to an end, here and now."

The magical glow dissipated altogether, and the figures came completely into view.

"No, dear sister," replied the blackguard, "it has only just begun."

Alhandra and Jozan stepped into the melee, accompanied by two holy warriors, each wearing the symbol of the god Heironeous.

A warm flush of pride and hope washed over Regdar, filling him with strength and confidence. He gripped his sword tightly in his good hand, dislodged it with a mighty tug, and lunged at the nearest soldier. The tip of the blade slipped across a metal plate on the man's splintmail and lodged in the leather padding underneath. The big fighter dropped his shoulder and put weight behind the strike.

"This is for Clemf," he said, and the tip plunged through hardened leather into soft flesh.

The man screamed and let go of his weapon, reaching with both hands to try to pull Regdar's sword out of his belly. He didn't need to, as Regdar wrenched it free himself, shouting, "Two!"

With the backswing he decapitated the last of Clemf's killers and roared, "Three!"

The swirling blue-white of the teleportation circle faded from Jozan's eyes, and he took in the grand melee before him. Regdar and his crew were badly outnumbered. The four new arrivals didn't even the balance, but Alhandra and her holy avengers resolutely advanced to deal with the blackguard.

Jozan went to save his friend Regdar.

A semicircle of armored warriors surrounded the man.

"You never did learn when to retreat," he said, knowing that even if Regdar could hear him, he wouldn't listen anyway.

The cleric stepped up to the first black-armored warrior he encountered and placed his hand on the man's shoulder. His fingers glowed as they touched the metal plates of the splintmail. At first contact, his spell discharged, flooding into the warrior. All the muscles in the man's body constricted, and he exhaled as if being crushed, then collapsed to the ground.

A handful of the soldiers menacing Regdar turned their attention to the newly arrived cleric.

Jozan lifted the mace from his belt. "May Pelor see fit to look after your immortal souls," he recited as he hammered the head of his weapon against a warrior's helm.

"Moradin works in mysterious ways," said Whitman between swings of his massive hammer. His arms were growing tired, but the sight of the cleric, the paladin, and their holy avengers filled him with a needed boost of strength.

So far he'd considered himself lucky. His enchanted elven chain armor blocked at least a half-dozen scimitar attacks that he'd been unable to parry with his hammer. He was cut a few times, but he still had his head, both feet, and two hands. Though he figured a good dwarf was worth at least three jann any day, he had to admit that this particular fight had involved more luck than skill.

"Just not in the dice for me today," he said, slamming down the head of his hammer on a janni's foot.

The outsider gave a terrific roar, then returned the blow with its scimitar. The fine blade descended, and Whitman watched it come in. Twisting sideways, the dwarf let the weapon slip down his belly, skidding harmlessly off the worked metal rings of his armor and sliding all the way to the floor.

The janni overbalanced and had to bend forward to keep hold of its sword. Whitman kicked up, catching his foe in the gut. The burly outsider blew out all the air in its lungs in a singular, uncontrolled belch, and let go of its sword, opting instead to protect its ribs.

The janni balanced for a moment, bent forward as it was, wobbling a bit back and forth. Then, almost as if it were moving in slow motion, it tumbled backward, landing first on its ass, then on the back of its head.

No longer surrounded, Whitman tumbled one full revolution away from the other two jann. When he came to his feet, he brought his hammer up before him and smiled at his otherworldly opponents.

"Now," he said, tapping the head of his weapon in his muscular palm, "if either of you have any wishes left, I suggest you use them to get your sorry butts out of here before I turn you into genie paste."

Tasca touched the wound on his face. He pulled his hand away and examined the blood, then he looked up at Lindroos and smiled.

"I think," he said, "that a scar on my cheek will only make me more rakishly attractive." He polished his fingernails against his chest. "I should thank you. Women love scars." He chuckled. "You of all people should know that."

When a loud boom echoed through the room and a glowing sphere of light erupted in the opposite corner, the blackguard turned around. Tasca didn't hesitate before leaping for his bow.

In one bound he made it to the spot and scooped up the weapon. He spun, an arrow already nocked to its string, prepared for the blackguard and whatever new monstrosity was inside that magical cylinder.

He was pleasantly surprised. Instead of the gibbering horror or pit fiend he had expected to see, a trio of Heironeous's holy warriors were advancing on Lindroos, and a cleric of Pelor was rushing up to help Regdar.

"Well, well," said the elf, letting his arrow fly across the room. "The gods are fickle indeed."

Regdar fought with renewed strength. Behind the line of killers surrounding him, his old friend Jozan was also bashing heads.

"Not quite the same as killing goblins, eh cleric?" Regdar

shouted over the noise of battle. His greatsword sliced into a soldier's arm, cutting it off at the elbow. Reversing directions, he chopped at another.

"No," came the reply from Jozan. "At least we don't have Lidda to worry about this time." His mace collided with another man's skull. The warrior went down in a heap.

Regdar replied, "What I wouldn't give for her quick wit and quicker sword right now."

"Me, too," admitted Jozan. "Me, too."

Alhandra and her two holy avengers stood before Lindroos, their swords at the ready.

"I'd give you a chance to surrender, sister," said the paladin, "but I know too well that you'd rather do this the hard way."

Lindroos nodded. "Naturally."

"I don't know how you managed to survive your trip to the Elemental Plane of Fire, but this time, I'll finish you myself." Alhandra charged her sister, the two holy warriors at her side.

Lindroos gave ground before the holy warriors as they came on. In her retreat, the blackguard lifted a small, ornately carved horn to her lips and gave it a sharp blow. A deep bellow issued forth. Thick, soupy vapor poured out of the instrument to roll over the lip and drift toward the floor.

At the sound of the horn, the warriors arrayed around the room turned away from their combats without hesitating a blink and flocked to their mistress. Their stampede shook the floor, and the noise of their booted feet echoed from the walls.

The jann, too, heeded the call by flying up toward the ceiling, leaving the angry, hammer-wielding dwarf far below. They crossed the room in a heartbeat and landed between the blackguard and her pursuers.

Alhandra put her hand up, staying her holy avengers. The trio stopped and turned toward the crowd of oncoming soldiers, letting Lindroos continue to run.

The blackguard blew again on her horn. The dense fog poured out, quicker now. In moments she was surrounded by her minions and by a growing, opaque cloud. As a group, the soldiers and jann backed into the fog, slowly disappearing from view.

Regdar and Jozan crossed the room to stand beside Alhandra. The elf and dwarf followed suit. Together they formed a line, seven warriors against perhaps twice their number.

Lindroos was concealed by the fog at this point up to her shoulders. She took in another breath and blew again, filling the corner of the room.

"I'd say it was nice to see you again, sister," she said, "but I know how you feel about lies." The fog drifted above her head, obscuring her completely from view.

The still-growing fog bank reached out in drifting tendrils, devouring the retreating gang of evil warriors. Alhandra looked back at Regdar and his men. They were all wounded, dripping blood from multiple wounds. Over the big fighter's shoulder, the paladin caught sight of Naull, her crumpled body lying in a heap in the middle of the room.

She looked back at the growing cloud. Lindroos and her soldiers were inside, but who knew what sort of evil was concealed in those fumes. Alhandra was seasoned enough to know that there was magic in this world that would harm only the good and pure of heart while sparing the wretched and wicked.

She turned to her holy avengers. "We've won this battle," she said. "Let her go."

18

Regdar knelt beside Naull. "No, Jozan," he explained. "She was with the blackguard willingly." He looked up at the cleric and shrugged. "She said she was angry that I left her in the City of Fire."

"Angry that you left her?" asked Alhandra. "She asked you to go."

"That's how I remember it," replied Regdar. "She must be under a spell."

Jozan knelt beside him and took hold of Naull's wrist. He nodded his head. "I don't think it was a spell," he said. "There are few things that can compel a person to act so violently toward someone they consider a friend."

"Jozan is right, Regdar," agreed the paladin. "As powerful as Lindroos is, there are only a handful of wizards in this part of the world who could even cast a spell that would make Naull act the way you describe." She examined the wound on Tasca's face as she spoke.

Regdar dropped his head. "What if she no longer considers me a friend?"

Jozan looked up from his patient on the floor. "I've seen some interesting wounds caused by women who had a particular hatred for the men they once loved," said the cleric. "Even assuming Naull did blame you for leaving her in the City of Fire, I don't sense that her spirit turned to evil."

Regdar crinkled his brow. "I don't understand."

Jozan smiled. "Even if she hated you now, Naull is still a good person at heart, and she wouldn't harm you if she were under a spell."

The big fighter slumped even more. "Then what made her act like that?"

"Knowing Lindroos," said the paladin, "it's likely a curse."

Jozan looked at Alhandra. He cocked his head to the side, seeming to ponder the idea, then he nodded.

"She could be right."

Regdar looked up. "Can you cure her?"

Jozan took a deep breath and nodded. "Yes," he said, "but I need time. There are prayers and rituals. . . ."

"Then I suggest we get ourselves safely outside of this tainted fortress and find a good camp for the night," said Alhandra. "You men are in need of some serious healing and rest."

Regdar nodded. He slipped his hands under Naull's limp body and stood up. Her petite frame draped over his outstretched arms as if she were a child's doll. He looked to Whitman and Tasca.

"You two bring Clemf." He lowered his head, taking a deep breath to steady his emotions. "We'll give him a proper burial when we're out of this godforsaken place."

Outside the swamp, far from the shadow of Mt. Fear, Regdar piled one last shovelful of dirt onto Clemf's grave.

"I'm sorry, my friend," he said. "I never imagined it would be this way."

With a final sigh, he turned and headed back to the campfire where Jozan was finishing healing Whitman and Tasca.

"You're next, Regdar," said the cleric.

Regdar nodded and sat down near the fire. Jozan knelt beside him.

"What should we do with Naull?" asked the fighter as the cleric examined him. "She's been unconscious for a while, but she'll wake up soon. I hit her awfully hard."

Jozan prodded the wound in Regdar's shoulder. "Well," he said, "without knowing exactly how she's been cursed, I think it would be best if we tied her up and gagged her, so she can't use her magic. Maybe even put a guard on her."

Regdar clenched his eyes shut against the pain as Jozan worked. "I'll stay up with her."

The cleric nodded. "I had a feeling you'd say that."

The moon rose high in the sky that night, illuminating the open plain. A light wind blew the razor grass and dried vegetation, making a rustling sound all round. The fire burned low in the pit, hissing and popping now and again.

Regdar looked down on Naull. She lay on her side, hands tied behind her back, a torn piece of cloth tied around her mouth.

He shook his head. "I'm so sorry," he whispered. "So very sorry."

Naull rolled to one side and straightened her legs. She groaned, then blinked her eyes open. Regdar knelt in front of her, hoping that somehow she'd wake to see him and everything would be like it had been before.

The wizard tugged on her restraints, but they didn't budge.

Straining without the use of her hands, Naull sat up. When her eyes crossed Regdar, they narrowed into a glare that made the man shiver. He felt like a child again, caught by a parent after doing something terribly wrong and being judged for a mistake he would never live down.

"Naull," he said sheepishly, "please believe that I didn't want to leave you."

She continued to glare.

"The city was shifting back into the Elemental Plane of Fire. You were trapped with Lindroos in the magical sphere that you created. You asked me to go, to save myself." Regdar wrung his hands together, pleading with Naull. "I didn't want to go. Don't you remember? The others, they dragged me away. Krusk nearly killed me to get me away." He dropped his hands and his head.

"When we got outside the city, I . . . I didn't know what to do. I thought you were dead, and if you were then I wanted to die too. I wanted to rush back inside." He shrugged his shoulders, still looking at the ground. "I tried to go back, but the gates to the city slammed shut on me. Alhandra and the others urged me to travel with them, to go back to New Koratia, but I didn't. I stayed there for days, wishing I could see you one last time . . . agonizing over the pain and suffering you must be enduring, burned alive on the Plane of Fire. It pains me now to even think about it, about the suffering I felt for you." Regdar looked up.

Naull's gaze hadn't softened.

"I waited there almost two weeks," he continued, "hoping by some miracle that the city would return, or that you'd appear and everything would be okay." He snorted. "I couldn't believe you were really gone. I didn't want to believe you were gone." Taking a deep breath, the big fighter sat down hard on the dirt. "Finally, a gypsy caravan traveled past. I was dirty and hungry and probably didn't smell too good. They gave me some food and water and pointed me toward home. I don't remember the journey. When I arrived in New Koratia, I was lost. I was home, but I didn't belong. I had no purpose, no reason to live." He put his head in his hands.

"Had I known you were alive, I would have scoured the earth." He picked up a pile of dirt and let it fall through his hands. "Instead I volunteered for every dangerous mission, hoping to get myself killed in battle." He picked up a small rock and tossed it into the slowly receding darkness. "I hoped an umberhulk or ogre would smash my head in, but I was too afraid to let it actually happen." He shook his head again. "I'm sorry Naull. I'm so very, very sorry." Regdar's throat tightened up again, and tears welled up in the corners of his eyes. He sniffled, trying to hold it back.

A strong hand grabbed him by the shoulder, and Regdar scrambled to his feet, pulling his greatsword from its sheath as he did. Standing there, sword in hand, tears dripping down his face, his heart sounding like goblin war drums in his ears, Regdar looked into Jozan's smiling face.

He held his hands up. "Relax," said the cleric. "It's almost morning, and I'm ready to cast that spell."

Regdar lowered his sword. "Thank Pelor."

Jozan stood before Naull. The wizard glared up at him with the same angry expression she'd been using on Regdar.

"This won't hurt a bit," said the cleric. "May the good lord Pelor protect and look after your soul, and may he see fit to grant me the power to heal that which afflicts you." With that, Jozan leaned down and touched Naull on the forehead.

A slight breeze picked up, and Regdar could have sworn that, for a brief moment, he heard a choir singing.

Naull's eyes rolled back into her head, and something clicked audibly. A thin wire bracelet, the same color as the wizard's skin, came undone from her ankle and fell to the ground.

Jozan picked it up. "Well, well," he said. "Looks like it wasn't a curse after all, but a cursed anklet."

Regdar ignored him. He knelt beside Naull and undid her gag.

"Regdar," she said breathlessly, the word drifting from her lips as if she thought she'd never have the opportunity to say it again. "I knew you'd save me."

The fighter undid the restraints holding her hands. Naull sprang forward, wrapping her arms around him and nearly knocking him flat on his back.

"Thank the gods," she said into his ears, squeezing his neck tighter than a cloaker. "I thought I'd never get away from the blackguard or be able to tell you—" Naull leaped away from Regdar and began blurting out words faster than her tongue could form them. "Lindroos wants bottle. She's going to New Koratia. City of Fire. The efreeti—"

Alhandra stepped forward, trying to decipher what the wizard was saying.

Regdar put his hand on Naull's shoulder. "Slow down," he said. "One word at a time."

Naull looked at him and took a deep breath, then she smiled and continued. "Lindroos is heading to New Koratia," she explained. "She's looking for a jeweled bottle, one that was recently discovered in the ruins of Old Koratia."

Regdar's heart skipped a beat. "What?"

"She must be talking about the bottle we retrieved," explained Whitman, sitting near the fire behind the big fighter.

Regdar turned around, ready to tell the dwarf to shut up, but he decided it wasn't worth the argument and turned back to Naull.

"Why does she want the bottle?"

Naull took another breath. "When we encountered Lindroos in the City of Fire, she was after the key to the city. Remember? She wanted to bring the city out of its pocket dimension and into this plane. Once it was here, and she had the key, she could control the elemental forces of fire." She squeezed Regdar's arm. "Our intervention stopped her from getting it that day, but she's still determined to retrieve it. Problem is, the city's still on the Elemental Plane of Fire, and we shut the portal that can bring it back to this world."

Regdar scratched his head. "If you two managed to survive on the Plane of Fire, why didn't she just retrieve the key while you were there?"

"We never got there," she explained. "While the city was in transit, Lindroos pulled out a bone staff of some kind and snapped it in half. After that she grabbed hold of my shoulder, and we were transported to some terrible place—" Naull squeezed her eyes shut and shook her head. "The key was still in the city."

A tear came to her eye, and Regdar rubbed his hand against her cheek. "Please," he said. "Continue if you can."

Naull wiped the tear away. "Wherever we were, it must have been what Lindroos calls home. I think the bone was some sort of magical calling device, something she'd worked up long before in case of an emergency." She shrugged. "I never found out exactly, but in any case, we never made it to the Plane of Fire and—"

"I'm certain your time with my sister was a terrifying experience," interrupted Alhandra, "but we're getting off track. Why does Lindroos want the bottle?"

Naull nodded. "Imprisoned inside is a janni vizier."

"What does Lindroos want with a janni vizier?" interrupted Alhandra. "Wishes?"

"No, not at all," replied Naull, obviously irritated at being verbally prodded by the paladin. "Thousands of years ago, the vizier devised another way to access the City of Fire—a way that didn't require the city to be in this world and would allow a mortal to survive on the Elemental Plane of Fire indefinitely without being burned to a crisp. When the elemental masters discovered what the vizier was up to, they imprisoned her in that bottle."

"Pardon my ignorance," said Jozan, "but why would a janni vizier need a portal to the Elemental Plane of Fire? Genies can transport themselves to any of the elemental planes at will, and to my knowledge they don't even suffer from the climate."

"You're right," answered Alhandra, "but while the city is on the Plane of Fire, it's not accessible to just anyone. It was originally built to imprison a very powerful efreeti. Getting to the Plane of Fire isn't the problem, its getting into the impregnable city itself."

Regdar suddenly understood. "So Lindroos wants the key, and the vizier can help her get it. She wants a prisoner to help her get into a prison."

"Right," said Naull. "The vizier in the bottle knows how to get inside the City of Fire."

"So she can get in and back out with the key," said Jozan, the look of comprehension spreading across his face. "Then she can open the portal from this side."

"Not only that," explained Naull, "but the vizier will be indebted to Lindroos for freeing it. She'll have access to the elemental forces of fire to do with as she pleases, and a powerful friend who owes her one."

The group stood in stunned silence for a long moment.

"But what about the efreeti inside the city?" asked Jozan finally. "Does Lindroos have some way of taming it?"

Naull shrugged. "It's no longer in the city. Once the vizier managed to find a way in, the efreeti had a way out. The prison remains, but the prisoner is long gone."

"Okay, fine, fine," said Regdar shaking his head. "Evil people making evil plans. I get that part. What I still don't understand is how this has anything to do with you and me."

Naull smiled and wrapped both of her hands around his.

"Convenient revenge," she said. "Lindroos kept me as a slave since last we met, but when she discovered that you had taken the janni's bottle from her agent—"

"She decided to kill two birds with one stone," finished Regdar.

"Or two humans," corrected Whitman.

"Yes, yes," said the paladin, "but where is she now?"

Regdar's heart sank. "She's headed for New Koratia to take the bottle from the duke."

The group walked for two days straight, barely stopping long enough to rest and heal. The sun rose on the third morning as they approached their destination.

"We'll be able to see the eastern wall of New Koratia just over this rise," explained Regdar.

With Regdar in the lead and Whitman and Tasca flanking him, they marched to the top of the small hill and stopped dead in their tracks.

Below the hill, the sun was just beginning to warm the fields outside New Koratia's easternmost wall. Heavy fog still clung to the ground in large patches, especially to the north and south, where the river entered the city.

Between several scattered copses of trees and the remaining low-lying clouds, a battle raged. An army of black-clad soldiers overran the field. They were accompanied by several units of jann, all bare chested and carrying huge scimitars. They brandished their weapons and fought against what Regdar could only assume was the entire New Koratian army.

In the middle, his blue and gold-guilded standard held high, his elite guard arrayed around him, stood none other than Duke Christo Ramas.

"He's taken the field himself," said Regdar, dismayed. "This is all my fault."

"He's not going to be happy to see us, is he?" asked Tasca.

"You never know," said Whitman. "I doubt he'd turn down a friendly hammer in a fight."

"Don't be so sure," said Regdar. "The duke can be a very stubborn man."

"What are you talking about?" asked Jozan.

Regdar shook his head. "Let's just say we didn't leave under ideal terms."

"Or perhaps you could say we left not knowing the terms," added Tasca.

Regdar rolled his eyes. "I'll explain later."

Jozan shrugged, and the group charged across the field, making a beeline to the duke. They made it to the back of the enemy's line without being noticed, and their swords cut into the black-clad cultists as though they were made of butter.

Whitman smashed heads with his hammer, Regdar's greatsword cleared a path, and Tasca and Naull stood at the back of the pack lobbing arrows and spells over their friends' heads. Beside this group of heroes, the holy warriors took their toll as well. Swords, maces, and the power of Pelor smote the forces of evil all around. Every enemy they slew brought them closer to the duke. His standard was still several hundred paces away, however, and they were separated by perhaps a couple thousand troops and jann.

As the battle raged, the sun continued rising over New Koratia, and the fog slowly burned off in the warming morning rays. With the disappearance of the low-hanging clouds, more of Lindroos's troops appeared. It was as if the willowy vapors coalesced into articulated minions of unholy fervor.

Where the black-clad army clashed with the New Koratian military, blood spilled and men died. Where the blackguard's troops attacked the duke's elite guard, swords slashed and heads rolled. Where Regdar and his band cut their way through the attacking forces, goodness triumphed over evil.

Still, the duke remained surrounded by a much larger force, and Regdar knew that Koratia had nothing in reserve. This battle would determine the fate of the duchy and Regdar's home, at least in the near future. More importantly, if Lindroos won, it could quite possibly determine the fate of the entire kingdom.

As they fought their way across the field, Regdar spotted the commander of the elite guard.

"Gohem," he shouted. "Captain Masters!"

The gnome followed the sound of the familiar voice. When his eyes landed on Regdar, he looked shocked and confused. Hesitating for a moment, Gohem looked around, then turned and gave an order to one of his lieutenants. The soldier nodded and began shouting to the troops.

The line of blue-and-gold garbed guardsmen shifted toward Regdar and his men. The jann and cultists between the two groups were squeezed like a spider between a beetle's pincers, and they fell quickly. The former New Koratian soldiers and their holy warrior counterparts were soon enveloped by the duke's elite guard. Whitman, Jozan, Alhandra, and the holy avengers took places in line with the other soldiers. Tasca and Naull stood behind, dropping arrows and spells on the attacking army. Regdar stepped back to talk with Gohem.

"I wasn't sure if you'd consider us friend or foe," admitted the human.

"I'm still not certain," replied Gohem as he shook Regdar's hand.

"Perhaps *you're* not," boomed a voice, "but I am." Duke Christo Ramas stepped up to the two captains. "Captain Masters," he ordered, "arrest this man and his companions." The duke pointed his ring-bedecked finger at Regdar.

The gnome nodded, then looked at Regdar with a resigned expression. "Men," he shouted, "you heard the duke. Arrest Captain Regdar and his companions."

In a blink Regdar, Tasca, Whitman, Jozan, Alhandra, and the two avengers were in custody. Regdar was held tightly by two soldiers, one on each arm. He let himself be taken without a struggle, leaving his hands open and loose at his sides. He dropped his greatsword to the ground.

Restrained as he was, Regdar turned to his lord. "Duke Ramas," he pleaded, "we've come to help you."

The duke narrowed his eyes and stepped toward Regdar. "You knew the consequences of your actions, but you left anyway," he shouted. "For all we know, you've joined forces with the army that's attacking us now. You could be a traitor. Captain Masters, tell me, what do we do to traitors?"

The gnome cleared his throat. "Sir, we hang them."

"You see, Regdar, we have well-established regulations for dealing with people like you."

"But sir . . ." Regdar tried to pull away, but the soldiers on his arms held him tight. "I know I disobeyed your orders, and my actions should be punished, but I swear to you, I am not a traitor." He tugged again, only to be rebuffed again. "We know what the blackguard has come for, and we've returned to help—to make up for my mistake." He shook his head toward Jozan and Alhandra. "If you won't believe me, at least listen to the cleric or the paladin. They had no part in my leaving. Surely their words should carry weight."

The duke scratched his beard and studied Jozan and Alhandra. He nodded. "Yes, I see you keep good company." He stepped up to Jozan. "Tell me then, good cleric, is Captain Regdar telling—"

The line of elite guardsmen surrounding the duke and the prisoners suddenly buckled. A flood of black-clad soldiers poured in, and behind them strode Lindroos, a long, black cape billowing out as she walked. The cultists and jann cleared a path before her, and she moved right through the New Koratian soldiers up to Duke Ramas. Lifting her enchanted black blade, she lunged forward.

Regdar watched the blackguard. Time seemed to slow down, and the sounds of the battlefield drifted away. Straining with every muscle in his body, Regdar struggled against his captors. The soldiers held his arms tight, but Regdar let out a tremendous yell. Summoning strength he never knew he had, he gave one last, desperate push. He could feel his face burn bright red with the exertion. Blood vessels popped out on his forehead and biceps. Then his arms slipped free of his captors' grasp, and Regdar sprang forward with all the force he mustered. His body was like an arrow launched at the blackguard.

In a blink, his shoulder collided with Lindroos's midsection. The blackguard hollered as she was hit, and the two warriors smashed into the ground with a loud bang, tumbling away from the duke in a pile of heavy armor and muscle.

Captain Masters reacted in an instant, running through two jann and a human soldier with three quick blows. The gnome turned and forced the duke back and away from the advancing attackers. The temporarily stunned guardsmen reacted to the actions of their captain and reformed their frontline, forcing the invaders back.

When Regdar and Lindroos came to a stop, Regdar sprang to his feet. His sword was still on the ground somewhere in the swirling collection of elite guardsmen. Without a weapon, he stepped back and clenched his fists, then looked at Lindroos. The blackguard rose to her knees, then slowly lifted herself up, appearing to be in no hurry. Unlike Regdar, she still had her sword.

"It's a pity," Lindroos said as she rose to her full height, "that my girlfriend didn't finish you off when she had the chance."

A bolt of crackling, purplish-blue energy arced over Regdar's shoulder to strike Lindroos squarely in the chest. The stunned blackguard dropped her sword and fell to her knees, shaking and twitching from the lightning blast.

Naull stepped up beside Regdar. "I wasn't your girlfriend," she shouted. Then she grabbed the big fighter by his elbow and pulled him back toward the elite guardsmen.

Naull and Regdar crashed through the frontline, stumbling through a small gap the soldiers opened for them. They came to a stop only a few feet from the fighting. Regdar looked up to see Whitman, Tasca, Alhandra, and Jozan. All of them had been freed and were armed.

Beside them stood Duke Christo Ramas. The old fighter glared at Regdar for a minute.

"I should make an example out of you for disregarding my authority," he said, obviously perturbed, "but I have bigger problems right now." He ran his hand across his face. "Fighting against impossible odds has always been your forte."

A lull in the fighting brought an eerie quiet over the center of the battlefield. Lindroos pulled her forces back to regroup. The elite guardsmen hadn't given chase, instead holding their line to protect the duke. At the edges of the open field outside of New Koratia, the battle raged on.

Regdar looked across the field at the blackguard and her slowly forming unit of soldiers and jann. He turned to Alhandra.

"What do you think she's up to?"

The paladin shrugged. "Evil. What else?"

"I mean, besides the obvious."

"Well," replied Alhandra, "my guess is that with the backing of the jann, she didn't expect to encounter this much trouble with the army of New Koratia." The paladin turned and looked Regdar in the eye. "She's probably all out of plans, and now she's improvising." She put her free hand on his shoulder. "Which makes her very unpredictable and even more dangerous."

Regdar nodded. "You know her better than any of us," he said. "What should we do?"

Alhandra looked over the battlefield. "We wait for her to make the next move. If she's making this up as she goes along, that means she's out of surprises."

As if Lindroos had heard their conversation, she and her newly reformed unit charged. Regdar could hear their booted feet pounding the hard ground as they advanced, and he could feel the soldiers around him tensing up.

Tasca fired two arrows, then his string went silent. He dropped his bow and empty quiver on the ground and unsheathed his rapier. Whitman stood beside him, a grim smile on his face. The head of his hammer rested casually on the ground with both his hands wrapped around the hilt.

"You know, Whitman," said Regdar, studying the smirk on the dwarf's face, "someone who didn't know you might think you were enjoying yourself."

The dwarf shifted his glance to look at the human out of the corners of his eyes. "Someone who did know me would know that I am."

The first four jann leading the charge impacted the front of the duke's line, and the sounds of battle filled Regdar's ears. Metal screeched as it bent and was ripped open. Men screamed as their guts were torn from their bodies. Grunts of exertion and the clang of weapons colliding mingled into a new sound, startling in its familiarity and unnerving in its foreignness.

Then the sky began to darken. At first Regdar thought it was rain clouds or the beginning of some magical effect. Looking up, he saw a dozen jann flying high into the sky, each of them holding one of the duke's elite guardsmen in his grasp. A chill ran down Regdar's spine as he realized what was happening. In the next heartbeat, the jann dropped their captives, hurling them like stones from the height of a castle wall.

Bodies rained down on Regdar and his men. Several New Koratian soldiers were hit by the grisly bombs, smashed into piles of goo by their falling comrades. The sounds turned Regdar's stomach. He was almost grateful for the screams of horror that nearly drowned out the sounds of impact.

Another host of jann lifted off into the sky. This time the soldiers fought back.

"You're coming down with me, bottle boy," shouted an elite guardsman as he soared into the air.

The man jammed his dagger deep into the janni's stomach when they were no more than ten feet in the air. The outsider growled and let the man fall back to the ground unhurt.

Others weren't so lucky. As more bodies plunged earthward, the elite guardsmen broke their ranks to get away from the danger zone, and enemy soldiers flooded through the gap. What once had been an orderly, organized resistance turned into a frenzy of individual fights. Pockets of guardsmen fought against cultists and their jann counterparts. As men scattered everywhere, Lindroos marched forward through the chaos.

Regdar grabbed Whitman and Tasca. "Protect the duke," he shouted, and the three warriors turned around.

As they closed in on the duke, another body fell to the ground before them. The heavily armored soldier crashed into the only organized unit in the area—the duke and his personal bodyguards. A number of guardsmen were struck down, and those who remained were watching the sky as much as the ground.

A handful of black-clad soldiers closed in to attack. The guardsmen were outnumbered and shaken, their ranks diminished and demoralized by horror. Regdar watched the duke draw his own weapon and wade into the fight.

Three of Lindroos's men crowded the duke. The old warrior narrowed his eyes and whipped his keenly honed, magical battle-axe around in three quick, perfect strikes. Three cultists dropped to the ground, each in his turn—one with a head wound, another with a freshly opened belly, and the third missing his privates. The sight of the old man laying waste to a pack of evil soldiers brought a smile to Regdar's face.

"That's why he's the duke," said Regdar as they closed in.

"No," said Whitman, lifting his hammer, "he was born to the title."

Tasca shook his head, looking at Regdar. "It's a dwarf thing."

The three fighters fought through the crowd of enemy warriors. They covered ground quickly. The duke mowed down enemies on all sides. Regdar, Whitman, and Tasca cut up anyone wearing black who stood in their path. In less than a minute they fought through the last line of evil soldiers separating them from the duke.

Several paces away, Captain Masters was joined by Jozan, Alhandra, and one of the holy avengers—Regdar didn't see the other one anywhere.

"Seems you have things under control, my lord," Regdar said, admiring the duke's bloody axe.

The duke smiled. "Did you think I carried this beautiful axe just for show?"

Over the duke's shoulder, the air shifted and wavered, rippling like the surface of a pool disturbed by a tossed stone. A form took shape rapidly out of the shimmering air and wrapped its arms around the duke.

"Janni," shouted Regdar. He grabbed one of the outsider's arms and tried to pry it off the duke.

The genie jerked away, pulling itself and the duke out of Regdar's reach, then it launched into the air, taking the duke along.

Tasca bent his legs and leaped, dropping his rapier in the process. The elf soared high over the other guardsmen's heads and grabbed hold of the janni's foot. The monster's ascent slowed from the added burden. The bare-chested outsider glared down at the elf dangling from its ankle. It shook the leg, trying to kick off the unwanted passenger.

Meanwhile the duke struggled against the janni's grip. Shifting his weight from side to side, the old fighter slowly slipped down through the outsider's arms. Between Tasca hanging from its foot and the duke's flailing, the janni had a hard time keeping its balance in flight. The trio twisted sideways in the air. Duke Ramas slipped free of the janni's arms, and Regdar bolted forward.

Regdar hoped only to break the duke's fall somehow, but before the man struck the ground, another janni swooped in and grabbed him from the air, then surged back up toward the clouds.

Regdar stopped only a step from where the duke would have landed. He watched in growing anger as the janni flew with the duke toward the eastern wall of New Koratia. In the distance, Regdar could make out another janni hovering above the city, a figure in its grasp as well. He squinted.

"Is that—?"

"Lindroos," said Alhandra. She stepped up beside him and was looking at the same janni. "Yes, it is she."

"Then she has the duke." Regdar looked around, taking stock of the situation. The fighting had slowed. The final surge made by the invaders was no more than a last ditch effort to grab the duke. When Lindroos left the field, the jann also departed. Deprived of their leader and their strongest shock troops, the cultists were no match for the rallying New Korations. Most were already dead, in custody, or fleeing for their lives.

Naull ran up, pointing at the duke and Lindroos, both being flown over the wall of the city by jann. "We can't let her get that bottle."

Regdar nodded. "When I retrieved it, the duke seemed quite relieved to have it in his possession. I'm sure it's well hidden."

"Still," said Alhandra, "Lindroos can be quite persuasive. We need to get to her before she gets to him, or retrieve the bottle ourselves."

Regdar agreed. "But who knows where he's hidden the bottle?

The keep is a labyrinth. Something as small as a bottle could be anywhere. Just finding the duke and Lindroos could take us days."

"The bottle is in a warded vault," said a voice.

Regdar turned to see Captain Masters nursing a wounded leg as he limped toward him. "It's in his bedroom, behind the picture of King Ramas."

"Put me down there," commanded Lindroos, pointing to a spot in the courtyard. "Near the door."

The janni did as Lindroos commanded, setting her down gently before the door on the edge of the courtyard inside the ducal palace. The other janni set the duke down next to her.

The minute Duke Ramas had his feet on the ground, Lindroos punched him in the face, and the duke fell backward.

Lindroos nodded to the jann. They proceeded to disarm the old, fallen fighter.

"I want you to understand, Ramas," said the blackguard, pacing before him, testing the sharpness of her blade as a chef might test her cleaver, "I have no qualms about killing you." She leaned down, smiling in his face. "In fact, I think I'd enjoy it."

Christo Ramas simply nodded.

Lindroos stood up. "Good," she said. "As long as you play along and behave, there's no reason for me to torture or maim you." She pointed the tip of her sword at him. "You don't want to be maimed, do you Ramas?"

The duke shook his head.

The jann stepped back, taking the duke's weapons and most of his armor with them.

"You two stay and guard this entrance," she ordered. "The duke is going to show me where he's keeping our friend trapped inside a terribly cramped bottle."

Regdar's lungs burned inside his chest. He'd never run so far so fast, wearing heavy armor, in all his life. He tried to distract himself by looking at the things around him. The ground was littered with dead or dying soldiers—that didn't make him feel any better. Beside him, Tasca and Whitman ran at full speed.

Whitman was having a hard time of it, trying to keep up. With his typical determination and his teeth gritted tight, the dwarf carried on, charging toward New Koratia with all of his strength. His boots of speed helped briefly, but in the end it was Whitman's willpower that allowed him to stay with the elf and the human.

Tasca, on the other hand, made the run seem effortless. He smiled when Regdar looked at him. Then he shrugged, obviously responding to the look of confusion on Regdar's face. The elf was as composed and casual as a princess at a harvest festival.

The eastern wall of the city came up quickly. Regdar felt as if he'd never make it, and he'd never been so happy to be wrong. The arched entranceway was completely unguarded. The group headed into the city, toward the bridge from the Merchants' Quarter over the river to the duke's island keep.

Under normal circumstances, Regdar would have expected to be stopped at several checkpoints along their route. Security getting over the River Delnir onto the island in the middle of New Koratia was always tough. Being attacked by an army of mercenaries and genies was hardly normal circumstances for the trading city.

Duke Ramas limped down the long, dark corridor.

"Move it, Ramas," ordered Lindroos, jabbing the tip of her blackened blade into his back. The jann had removed the duke's chestplate, leaving only a linen shirt between the weapon and his skin.

Christo stumbled forward, pulling away from the blade but hopping gingerly on his injured leg. He turned and glared at the blackguard.

"I'm going as fast as I can," he said through gritted teeth. "If that bothers you, take it up with your goons who smashed up my leg."

Lindroos shoved him down the hall. "Tell your sob story to someone who cares," she said. "And keep moving."

Christo glared for a moment longer, his eyes locked with hers, then he turned and continued down the hall. He took three limping steps before Lindroos shoved him again. Skipping forward a step, he caught his balance, then reversed directions.

His elbow flew backward and smashed Lindroos in the nose. The sound of crunching cartilage was magnified by the narrow stone corridor, and blood trickled down the blackguard's face. With her arms flailing to her sides, she stepped back, touched a hand to her lip, then looked down on the crimson smear on her fingertips.

The duke wheeled around, pivoting on his good leg, and lifted his fists in front of his face—one slightly higher than the other, both right below his eyes. Setting his feet shoulder width apart, he braced himself for a fight.

Lindroos rubbed her wrist across her face, clearing most of the blood. Her nose pointed off in a different direction than it had only moments before. Lifting her sword, she pointed the tip at the duke.

"How valiant," she said. "Fighting an armed opponent with just your bare hands. I see why they made you duke." She punched a fist in the air, followed by a parody of a kick. "Did they teach you to box in aristocrat school?" she asked, laughing.

Christo lunged forward and jabbed with his right hand. His punch was blindingly quick, and it caught the mocking blackguard on the chin. Her head slammed back, and she almost lost her balance again.

Lowering her head, Lindroos rubbed the back of her neck and her cheek. After opening and closing her jaw several times, she turned her attention back to Christo.

"Okay, old man," she said, "I'm through being pleasant." With a quick feint to the right, Lindroos lunged and caught the duke in the crook of his right arm. Her sword opened a wound in his exposed bicep from elbow to shoulder.

Duke Ramas hissed and limped back. The wound bled freely. When he tried flexing his arm, he could see the slashed muscles moving across each other under the flow of blood. The pain made his vision grow narrow, so he let the arm hang straight down his side. With his good arm he steadied himself against the wall.

Lindroos stepped forward and punched him hard in the face with the pommel of her sword. The duke's knees went weak, and he collapsed onto the stone floor.

The blackguard leaned over the bleeding old warrior. "Don't make me kill you here," she said. Lifting her sword to the side of his head, she slashed off a piece of his ear.

Christo let out a cry and put his hand up to protect his head. Warm blood ran down the side of his neck. "If you kill me, you'll never get the bottle," he spat.

Lindroos leaned down and picked up the ragged bit of ear. "If I kill you, I'll take you apart bone by bone until you wish you'd never heard of that bottle," she hissed. "And I'll still find it, if I have to dismantle this city brick by brick."

Regdar slowed to a walk as he crossed over the bridge. They were close—close enough that he needed to catch his breath before the fighting began again. Two city blocks past the end of the bridge, the tall walls of the ducal palace rose imposingly into the air.

The fighter waved the group toward the northern corner. "There's a door to the courtyard there," he explained. "Going around to the front gate will take too long."

Tasca and Whitman nodded, heading for the portal they'd used so often. Jozan, Alhandra, and her remaining holy avenger followed close behind.

Naull stepped up close to Regdar. "Here," she said.

Reaching up and wrapping her hands behind his head, the wizard lifted herself up on her tiptoes and kissed the big fighter. After lingering on his lips for a long moment, she finally pulled away and spoke an arcane word. Her hands buzzed with power, and Regdar felt suddenly stronger.

"For luck," she said smiling.

Regdar curled his fist up toward his head. His biceps bulged. "Thanks," he said, smiling. "Now if you could only make that permanent."

"For that," replied Naull, "you'll have to stick around for a while."

The big fighter blushed. "Maybe I will."

"See that you do."

The rest of the group had already passed through the door. The clash of weapons drifted over the wall to the two lovers.

"Trouble," said Regdar, and he took off at a run, with Naull following close behind.

Inside the courtyard, Whitman and Jozan battled two jann. Alhandra and her holy avenger were trying to get into flanking positions, and Tasca stood in the rear, patiently waiting his turn to get at either of the outsiders.

As Regdar closed in, he watched Jozan take a step back and level his hands at one of the janni.

"Flee," he yelled, his voice booming above all other noise in the courtyard.

The janni dropped its weapon and jumped into the air, flying straight away from the cleric as fast and as directly as it could.

Lindroos looked down on Duke Christo Ramas. She kicked him in the face, and he sprawled across an elegantly woven rug.

She shook her head. "You have a nice room, Duke," she said, circling around him and sheathing her sword. "You live surrounded by such beautiful things. I can't believe you'd sacrifice all of this for a lousy bottle . . . that you don't even know how to use."

The duke struggled to his knees, and Lindroos kicked him again in the ribs. He coughed and collapsed to the floor, spewing blood and mucus.

The blackguard continued pacing around the room. "You have lovely paintings . . . nice furniture too." She stopped and feigned surprise. "And would you look at that," she said, pointing into an adjoining room. "Your bed is all the way over there, in a whole separate room of its own! Well I'll be."

Christo rolled onto his back. His face was bruised and badly swollen from the beatings. Rivulets of blood crisscrossed his face, both dried and fresh. He struggled to hold himself upright enough to see Lindroos as she paced around him.

"It must be nice to live amid all this luxury. So I'll tell you what," she said. "I'll let you keep living, and you can even keep all of these wonderful possessions, if you just tell me where that bottle is."

Christo coughed again, struggling to breathe, spitting blood and goo onto his soiled shirt. When he regained his composure, he glared up into her eyes and slowly shook his head.

"No," he said with a raspy voice.

Lindroos knelt in front of him. She grabbed the duke by his collar and lifted him to her face. "I've been more than patient with you, Ramas," she said in a cool, metered voice. "But this is the last time I will ask you." She pulled a dagger from her boot and held it against his throat. "Last chance now. Where ... is ... my ... bottle?"

Christo looked up at the blackguard with hatred plain on his face. He held her stare for a moment, then he shifted his gaze, breaking eye contact. His expression softened, and he dropped his head.

"You win," he said. "It's in the next room, behind a false wall, behind the bed." He pointed with his chin.

Lindroos smiled wide and dropped the duke to the floor. "It's about time," she said, turning and heading into the adjoining room.

Regdar pulled his greatsword out of the last janni. The creature convulsed then fell silent.

Waving his hand over his shoulder, he led the way into the palace. They wound through a series of long, stone hallways, then up a flight of stairs. Deep in the center of the palace, taking up almost a quarter of the second floor, they came to the duke's personal chambers.

Regdar slipped quietly through the open door with Alhandra close behind him and the others behind her. Inside, a huge, canopied bed dominated the floor. A painting of King Ramas hung behind it. At its foot, a set of double doors opened into a second room. Regdar heard a voice, and he held his finger up to his lips, further silencing the already quiet crowd.

Peeking around the corner of the open double doors, the big fighter saw the duke lying on his back—his face bloodied and bruised, his eyes swollen and narrow. Next to him knelt Lindroos. She held him by his collar.

"I've been more than patient with you, Ramas," she said. "But this is the last time I will ask you." She pulled a dagger from her boot and held it against his throat. "Last chance now. Where . . . is . . . my . . . bottle?"

The duke looked up at her, then he looked away. Regdar leaned out a little farther, catching the duke's gaze. When they made eye contact, the big fighter nodded.

The duke's eyes widened for a flash, then he dropped his head.

"You win," he said to Lindroos. "It's in the next room, behind a false wall, behind the bed."

Lindroos let go of the duke and stood up.

Regdar pulled back, hiding himself behind the doorframe. Alhandra stood right behind him, and he nudged her in the ribs, looking over his shoulder to give her a nod.

"It's about time," said the blackguard.

Regdar held his sword over his head, the tip pointed to the ground, both hands wrapped around the hilt. He took a deep breath and waited. His heart was pounding so loud in his ears he couldn't hear anything else.

A flash of black crossed into his field of view. Regdar heaved downward with every bit of magically enhanced strength he could muster. He heard himself roar as his greatsword descended. The tip hit metal and punched right through. He forced more strength behind the strike, and his feet lifted off the ground with the force of the blow.

Regdar's attack knocked Lindroos to the floor. His sword stabbed right through the blackguard's shoulder and into the wooden planking, pinning her to the floor like a giant bug.

Alhandra sidestepped Regdar and lifted her holy blade into the air.

"Heironeous, grant me the power to smite the wicked!" she

shouted, and her blade sliced down on Lindroos's neck.

The blackguard's helm clanked on the ground as her head rolled free of her shoulders.

Alhandra stared down at the body of her dead sister. "And may you see it in your heart to have pity on those who have fallen from grace," she said, finishing her prayer.

Epilogue ... Regdar, Tasca, and Whitman stood at attention outside the duke's office. The heavy doors creaked open, and a short, bald, heavyset man with glasses came out.

"The duke will see you now," he said, and he held the door open for the soldiers.

Inside, Duke Christo Ramas, now fully healed after several days, rest and the ministrations of at least five clerics, sat behind his desk. He glared at the men as they walked in.

Regdar stopped several paces from the edge of the desk and saluted. The dwarf and the elf did the same.

The duke saluted back. "You'll be happy to know that Hortoga Gendolin, the Grandmaster of the wizards' school at the Floating Crystal, has seen to it personally that the vizier's bottle will never be found again."

The duke stood and stepped around from behind his desk. "I suppose I owe each of you a debt of gratitude." He paced before them. "You did save my life." He stopped and studied each of them. "The fact remains, however, that you, Regdar," he pointed his thick finger at the big fighter, "directly defied my orders and abandoned your position in the New Koratian army to chase after a dead person." He wheeled on Tasca and Whitman. "And you two followed suit without so much as a peep."

Tasca opened his mouth to speak, but the duke's glare silenced him.

"I've heard your excuses," he said, "chief among them being your loyalty to Captain Regdar. I find them to be no more than juvenile finger pointing." He looked each of them squarely in the eye, one at a time. "You are responsible for yourselves and your actions at all times, regardless of what a superior officer tells you."

Regdar wrinkled his forehead. "But sir—"

"Silence," shouted the duke. "I know damned well that I'm contradicting myself." He walked back behind his desk and sat down. "Now you can see my dilemma. If it hadn't been for a few quick-thinking individuals, we never would have gotten out of that mess."

Duke Christo Ramas scratched his face and once more looked over the three men in turn. After a long moment of silence, he spoke again.

"Here's what I'm going to do. Tasca and Whitman, you will both be reinstated in the New Koratian military and given promotions to the rank of captain." The duke smiled. "Let's see how you like it when one of your men decides to blame his actions on you."

"Yes, sir. Thank you, sir," said the dwarf and the elf in unison.

"As for you Regdar, I will release you from custody and reinstate you at your old rank, under one condition."

Regdar nodded. "What condition is that, sir?"

"That you never tell anyone what you got away with." The duke smiled. "I can't have the troops thinking I'm soft."

Capture the thrill of D&D® adventuring!

These six new titles from T.H. Lain put you
in the midst of the heroic party as it encounters
deadly magic, sinister plots, and fearsome creatures.
Join the adventure!

THE BLOODY EYE

TREACHERY'S WAKE

PLAGUE OF ICE

THE SUNDERED ARMS

RETURN OF THE DAMNED

THE DEATH RAY
December 2003

Legend of the Five Rings

The Four Winds Saga

Only one can claim the Throne of Rokugan.

WIND OF JUSTICE
Third Scroll
Rich Wulf

Naseru, the most cold-hearted and scheming of the royal heirs, will stop at nothing to sit upon the Throne of Rokugan. But when dark forces in the City of Night threaten his beloved Empire, Naseru must learn to wield the most unlikely weapon of all — justice.

WIND OF TRUTH
Fourth Scroll
Ree Soesbee

Sezaru, one of the most powerful wielders of magic in all Rokugan, has never desired his father's throne, but destiny calls to the son of Toturi. Here, in the final volume of the Four Winds Saga, all will be decided.

December 2003

Now available:

THE STEEL THRONE
Prelude
Edward Bolme

WIND OF HONOR
First Scroll
Ree Soesbee

WIND OF WAR
Second Scroll
Jess Lebow

Tales of Dominaria

LEGIONS
Onslaught Cycle, Book II
J. Robert King

In the blood and sand of the arena,
two foes clash in a titanic battle.

EMPEROR'S FIST
Magic Legends Cycle Two, Book II
Scott McGough

War looms above the Edemi Islands, casting the deep
and dread shadow of the Emperor's Fist.

SCOURGE
Onslaught Cycle, Book III
J. Robert King

From the fiery battles of the Cabal, a new god has arisen,
one whose presence drives her worshipers to madness.

THE MONSTERS OF MAGIC
An anthology edited by J. Robert King

From Dominaria to Phyrexia, monsters fill the multiverse,
and tales of the most popular ones fill these pages.

CHAMPION'S TRIAL
Magic Legends Cycle Two, Book III
Scott McGough

To restore his honor, the onetime champion of Madara must
battle his own corrupt empire and the monster on the throne.

November 2003

The Avatar Series

New editions of the event that changed all Faerûn…and the gods that ruled it.

SHADOWDALE
Book 1 • Scott Ciencin

The gods have been banished to the surface of Faerûn,
and magic runs mad throughout the land.

TANTRAS
Book 2 • Scott Ciencin

Bane and his ally Myrkul, god of Death, set in motion a plot to seize
Midnight and the Tablets of Fate for themselves.

The New York Times best-seller!
WATERDEEP
Book 3 • Troy Denning

Midnight and her companions must complete their quest by traveling
to Waterdeep. But Cyric and Myrkul are hot on their trail.

PRINCE OF LIES
Book 4 • James Lowder

Cyric, now god of Strife, wants revenge on Mystra, goddess of Magic.

September 2003

CRUCIBLE: THE TRIAL OF CYRIC THE MAD
Book 5 • Troy Denning

The other gods have witnessed Cyric's madness
and are determined to overthrow him.

October 2003

FORGOTTEN REALMS

R.A. Salvatore's
War of the Spider Queen

Chaos has come to the Underdark
like never before.

New York Times best-seller!

CONDEMNATION, *Book III*
Richard Baker

The search for answers to Lolth's silence uncovers only more complex
questions. Doubt and frustration test the boundaries of already tenuous
relationships as members of the drow expedition begin to turn on each other.
Sensing the holes in the armor of Menzoberranzan, a new, dangerous threat
steps in to test the resolve of the Jewel of the Underdark, and finds it lacking.

Now in paperback!

DISSOLUTION, *Book I*
Richard Lee Byers

When the Queen of the Demonweb Pits stops answering the prayers of her
faithful, the delicate balance of power that sustains drow civilization crumbles. As
the great Houses scramble for answers, Menzoberranzan herself begins to burn.

INSURRECTION, *Book II*
Thomas M. Reid

The effects of Lolth's silence ripple through the Underdark and shake the drow
city of Ched Nasad to its very foundations. Trapped in a city on the edge of
oblivion, a small group of drow finds unlikely allies and a thousand new enemies.

October 2003

FORGOTTEN REALMS

The foremost tales of the FORGOTTEN REALMS® series, brought together in these two great collections!

LEGACY OF THE DROW COLLECTOR'S EDITION
R.A. *Salvatore*

Here are the four books that solidified both the reputation of *New York Times* best-selling author R.A. Salvatore as a master of fantasy, and his greatest creation Drizzt as one of the genre's most beloved characters. Spanning the depths of the Underdark and the sweeping vistas of Icewind Dale, Legacy of the Drow is epic fantasy at its best.

THE BEST OF THE REALMS
A FORGOTTEN REALMS *anthology*

Chosen from the pages of nine FORGOTTEN REALMS anthologies by readers like you, *The Best of the Realms* collects your favorite stories from the past decade. *New York Times* best-selling author R.A. Salvatore leads off the collection with an all-new story that will surely be among the best of the Realms!

November 2003